THE
ROBERT OLEN BUTLER

PRIZE STORIES

2008

THE
ROBERT OLEN BUTLER
PRIZE STORIES

2008

)•)

DEL SOL PRESS

WASHINGTON, D.C.

The Robert Olen Butler Prize Stories 2008

Copyright © 2008 by Del Sol Press. All rights reserved.

DEL SOL PRESS, WASHINGTON, D.C.

HTTP://WWW.DELSOLPRESS.ORG

PAPER ISBN: 978-1-934832-06-6

FIRST EDITION

COVER PHOTOGRAPH: "NO FUTURE"
© PHOTOGRAPHER: PHOTODESIGN | AGENCY: DREAMSTIME.COM

DESIGN & COMPOSITION BY JONATHAN WEINERT

CONTEST COORDINATION IN 2007-2008 BY NICOLE CORLEY

Publication by Del Sol Press/Web del Sol Association, a not-for-profit corporation under section 501(c)(3) of the United States Internal Revenue Code.

Contents ❦

The 2008 Prize Winner 🐝

Winter Memories of the Summer Bear 🐻

KIMBERLY WILLARDSON

MIDSUMMER

Sammi taylor bought a bear. most women sammi knew, near her *certain* age, want Manolo Blahnik shoes, boob jobs, emerald earbobs, Botox, secret lovers, brand-spanking-new SUVs, knee lifts, or remodeled granite kitchens with Viking stoves. But Sammi bought a brown bear.

FRIDAY NIGHT, LATE MAY

Sammi first thought she wanted a horse. An Arabian.

"I want to get a horse," Sammi told her husband, Paul, over martinis and appetizers at the Zink Lounge.

"Criminy," Paul answered. "Here we go." He was clicking through text messages on his cell phone, though he had turned the ringer off and vibrator on.

"I think it would help me," Sammi said. "Make me feel connected . . . healthier . . . more grounded."

Paul snorted. "You just want to slink around the grocery store wearing high black boots, jodhpurs, and a riding cap with a chin strap. Like that cunt Constance O'Donnel."

Sammi winced. He knew she hated that word.

"Not Constance. It's *Susan Connelly* that shows horses. Dressage, it's called."

Paul snorted again. "Susan Connelly, Susan Connelly. Is she the one that had the twat lift? Reclaiming her virginity or some such nonsense?"

Sammi wished she had a cigarette. Nine years without lighting up, and she still craved a cigarette whenever Paul was an ass. Over the years, she found herself longing for a cigarette more, rather than less, often.

"Maybe I'll just start smoking again."

"Smoking makes you stink. More wrinkled and yellow," Paul said.

"So what? I'm disappearing anyway."

"Whatever," Paul said.

Against her better judgment, Sammi ordered another martini. Perhaps that's what led to the dream.

THE DREAM

Sammi dreamed she saw Lord Byron on the Quiver Street bus. She recognized him right off by his bum leg and the bear, dressed in a tuxedo, sitting next to him.

"Thank the Goddess you're here," Sammi said to Lord Byron. "Ravish me," she said and feigned a swoon. Lord Byron just let her fall and continued reading the chapbook in his hand.

The bear handed her a bouquet of purple coneflowers and said, "Idaho."

When Sammi bolted awake, sweating, she realized her TV had been bathing her prone body with images from a Cirque du Soleil retrospective for hours.

EARLY JUNE

"What'cha doing, Ma?"

"Sitting here hating your dad," Sammi's mother answered.

"Is he still around?"

"I kick him out, but he keeps coming back."

"Let me talk to him."

"Naw. He's at the BlackJack table. And I'm getting ready for my yoga class."

Sammi paused to calculate what time it was in Las Vegas for those two incongruous activities to take place. But she gave up. Her parents always seemed to be in a different time zone than she was.

"Oh," Sammi said.

"What's up? You sound blue."

"I feel like I'm disappearing."

"We're all disappearing. Welcome to the human race," Sammi's mother snapped.

"No. Seriously. No one makes eye contact. No one will wait on me in the mall."

"Oh, wah, wah, wah. Get a job. Start up your dog-training business again."

"And I'm having weird dreams."

"What's so wrong with disappearing? Head for the wilds. You come from a long line of feral women, Sammi. Take advantage of it."

BY THE WAY

Paul knew *exactly* who Susan Connelly was. He'd been boffing her every chance he got for the past ten months. Since she recovered from her vaginal "lift." Her doctor called it the "Love Procedure."

JULY 5TH

Sammi called her uncle (Louie—the one who'd spent his adult life either in State Prison, or out finding new ways to get back in). Louie knew a friend of a friend who specialized in exotic animals.

This friend, Dutchie Rickshaw, lived in White Buffalo, Montana. When she heard Dutchie's name, she knew he was the man who could provide the perfect brown bear. She paid for both her and Uncle Louie's plane tickets out there.

JULY 10TH

Dutchie lived in a trailer on the edge of the National Bison Range. Dutchie gasped and wheezed as he talked through the care and feeding of the bear.

"His name's Bobo. Bobo Dilly," Dutchie said. "He's a bike-riding bear. Juggles a bit: balls, gourds, bowling pins. Nothing sharp, though. Stands on his head. Walks on his hands."

"Yes. I'll call him Bear," she said.

Dutchie eyed her through the smoke of his cigarette. Camel, no filter. Sammi wondered if the cigarette would ignite the oxygen tank sitting next to Dutchie's tipsy, Tartan-plaid recliner. Lung cancer. That's why Dutchie had to give up the bear.

"Circus bears have names. Oh, yeah. He does other tricks, too. Can't rightly remember now," Dutchie said. "Gotta have fish and lots of it, Sister. Got a fish market nearby?"

"Yes."

"Any pets?"

"Three cats. A German shepherd."

Dutchie lit a fresh cigarette from the end of his smoking one. "The cats will disappear," he said. "Let 'em go. Bobo will allow the dog. Might grow to love him. Too bad you don't have a horse. Bobo loves horses and horses love Bobo. Used to have a horse here. Thunder was her name. She could run like the Devil. Man, oh man, oh yeah. She had to go, too. Went with my lungs."

Waving away the arms they offered for support, Dutchie lurched outside and showed them around his property. The wild wind came down at them straight from the sky, as if aiming to shoot them like arrows to the core of the earth. Then it whip-snapped and shrieked up from the crackling grass, trying to lift them into the clouds. Sammi saw how the Blackfoot Indians came to learn from and worship the sky, which was crowded with feathery bison, crows, bodiless wings, horses pounding, empty angel robes, lizards leering, human faces laughing, and an indecipherable alphabet. The clouds were a perpetually unfolding opera with dozens of featured players. The wind screamed a thousand voices; the wind had much to say.

Sammi strained to translate what the voices were saying to her, but Dutchie was elbowing her and poking the toes of his old Tony Lamas at black-and-purple patties littering his yard's coarse turf. "Bear scat. See the huckleberries? Poor bear. No huckleberries where you're going. There's old Thunder's barn."

Compared to Dutchie's trailer, the barn was lavish with its clean-edged oak beams and scrolled iron gated stalls. The rich, sweet scent of hay, oats, and composting horse poop floated like an invisible cloud inside the barn. Thunder must have just left.

The bear stood one step inside the expansive barn, his eyes blinking rapidly, head turning this way and that, arms clasped behind his back, as if he were an old retired professor returned to a much-changed college quad. He whimpered low in his throat. Dutchie patted his back, rubbed his left shoulder. The tips of the bear's fur burnished copper in the late afternoon sunbeams pouring into the barn.

The bear was fifteen—middle-aged, like Sammi—so his life skills were pretty much rote by now. He was lumpy and saggy, like her. But then he had always been lumpy and saggy. Hunchbacked. He had no memory of erect posture, smooth young skin, firm tits and ass, and the sensuous promises moonlight mixed with whiskey and whispers provided. A circus bear, he'd never copulated. Not any that Dutchie mentioned. The bear didn't care about his loss of sex appeal. But he was grumpy, reflective, vaguely dissatisfied. Like her.

Dutchie needed an hour on the oxygen tank and six puffs from his asthma inhaler to get up enough strength to show her how to file the bear's nails and brush his teeth. "Gotta brush his teeth or the whole joint will stink. Use Tom's all natural toothpaste. He'll sit pretty for that."

"Yes," Sammi said.

Dutchie said he wouldn't let Bobo go until she proved she could brush the bear's teeth. He was amazed she got the floss between each sword of the bear's teeth on her first try.

"And that's it. He'll have you," Dutchie said, crying openly. "Ol' Bobo. Bobo Dilly. Gonna miss you so bad." Dutchie gently stroked the soft slope between the bear's eyes and the suede-like backs of his ears.

"I'll call and send pictures," she said.

"I won't be here, Sister," Dutchie rasped back. "Just give me three more days with him. Just three days. You gotta see Glacier Park. Head up to Grinnell Lake. In three days, I'll have Bobo sitting out front with his suitcase."

BACKGROUND

In Sammi's twelfth summer, her family vacationed at Lake Nippissing, Ontario, with another family. On the way, as the five children and two mothers slept, Sammi's father and Mr. Copeland, the other father, drank bottle after bottle of Carling Black Labels as they drove through the night. Their rented van ended up slowing and burping to a benevolent rest against soft shrubbery way off the road when her father dozed at the wheel. Whew, lucky. Very lucky. But he smashed out a rear taillight trying to disentangle the van, and then things got tense. The mothers spit curses and yelled at the fathers all through the dawn until they arrived at the tiny gas station marking the entrance to their campgrounds.

A strange scene greeted them. Men milling around an enormous cage—crammed into the back of a ramshackle pick-up truck—containing an angry bear with a steel-jawed trap clenched onto his leg. The bear's blood oozed and dripped from the slit between the truck bed and tailgate. A tall, thin man with red hair and a beard poked at the bear with a long tree branch and waved around a rifle.

Sammi's mother was slapping her father's face and head and kicking his shins as they raced each other around the station's parking lot. Mr. and Mrs. Copeland were shouting obscenities at each other in the front seat of the van. Sammi tried to pull the other four children away from the hideous sight of the frantic bear, who was now foaming and moaning, and the red-haired savage who was trying to pump up the silent crowd by crowing in a language unknown to the vacationers. Sammi turned away, perhaps to realize that she was deeply involved in the most stressful situation thus far of her young life and trying to figure out what to do next. Maybe she thought of how lucky she'd been that far.

When Sammi turned back, her father was shouting at the red-haired man. "Jesus Christ, cut it out, you son-of-a-bitch. Leave that poor bastard alone." The crowd murmured encouraging agreement, so her father grabbed at the man's rifle.

Maybe Sammi realized this was her father's attempt to deflect her mother's assault. Maybe Sammi was struck by the fact that it was the first time, but not the last, that she had ever seen her father cry. And perhaps she wondered: are the tears his concern for the bear, or for her mother's justifiable anger, his nearly tragic mistake at the wheel, or simply lack of sleep and too much beer? Maybe. Sammi can't remember that close.

But Sammi never forgot how she felt next. After her mother, suddenly forgiving her father enough to take up his sword, snatched the tree branch from the red-haired fiend and jammed it straight into his crotch, causing him to collapse forward and retch violently. The crowd cheered and her mother held up the branch triumphantly. Like Madame Defarge.

They all felt triumphant.

THREE DAYS

The journey to Grinnell Lake is mapped by magic words: Bitterroot Valley, Wild Horse Island, Kalispell, Going-to-the-Sun Road, Two Medicine Lake, Beargrass.

East Glacier Lodge buzzed with the dreadful news of a missing hiker: gone two days and hope had just about run out. He was an inexperienced hiker, a German tourist, who'd insisted on going it alone despite repeated warnings.

"Oh, he's gone. Yep. He's dead. The bears got him," the grizzled curator of the Blackfoot Art Gallery cheerfully told Sammi and Louie. He pointed out the small window of his trailer, which served as his home, the art gallery (slick prints, rain sticks, and animal skins), and the office for his teepee lodging business. Three couples—three men and three women—were taking turns trying to untie the flaps of one of the ten enormous teepees dotting the curator's vast landscape of purple prairie. The campers were attempting to just *see* the teepee flaps through the cold, lashing rain, as they simultaneously tried to hang onto their hoods and clutch their coat collars tight to their necks.

"I just pulled them off the mountain. Had to get my Jeep out to do it. They're from Belgium. None of 'em has ever hiked a wooded trail before now. But they come here with their oversized backpacks and cameras and cell phones. Cell phones don't work out here and the wind grabs those tall backpacks so easy and whooooosh," he gleefully slapped his palms together. "You get knocked off the mountain."

He beamed as he paused. "Thousands of miles just to sleep in a teepee and get pulled off the mountain. They don't get it. We ain't Disneyland. We got rules here. Rule Number One: Nature Wins."

He held up his pudgy index finger again as they left the gallery. "Remember Rule Number One."

WEST GLACIER

Sammi remembered Rule Number One and wondered why she didn't feel more fear, as she mounted the horse, Dollar, that would take her to Grinnell Lake.

"No camera?" the walnut-faced trail guide had asked her when he tied her sleeping bag and small backpack on the supply horse's back.

"Just the one in my head," she'd answered.

Uncle Louie didn't have a camera either, and he kept his pack on his own back, despite the guide's warning that it would soon get too heavy.

"We're a strange group," the guide said.

They were. Louie, dazed by the scenery or perhaps by whatever he was carrying in his backpack, said not one word the entire eight hours up the trail to Grinnell.

Sammi rarely spoke: just sometimes commenting on the neon blue mushrooms or orange lichen clinging to the old trees, or the huckleberry patties studding the trail.

"Bear respects horse and horse respects bear," the guide told them, "But, if they should happen to meet, the horses will let you know for sure. Bears haunt Grinnell; it's one of their favorite spots."

This didn't frighten her, either. After a few hours on the horse, her butt was screaming in agony, but she wouldn't allow herself to complain out loud. She focused on the ferns and flowers and clouds. The occasional mountain goat and hawk.

Perhaps it was the altitude, lack of humidity, the purple sage's incense, or the peculiar intensity of the sky's blue. Whatever, Sammi couldn't dredge up one single fear or concern. Even after looking into the turquoise mirror of the perfect lake—relishing the relief of being off the horse's back, kneeling on solid ground—and seeing her sunburnt, aging face gazing back at her, she didn't get upset. She'd just spent eight hours on horseback, slipping and sliding on creekbed slate or clip-clopping through the cool forest shadows. She expected bears, goats, and moose. She came to expect even elves or dryads. She expected something momentous and magic: that her face had changed to become more beautiful, younger, or just wise. But no. The same suspicious eyes, turned-down mouth, and wrinkles, ringed by graying hair, looked back at her when she knelt over the lake.

The guide hurried them from the lake edge. He had been recruited via radio to help search for the missing hiker, though it was impossible he'd be this far from East Glacier.

"Want to help search?" he asked her.

Sammi wasn't surprised to find that she did, indeed, want to help search. But Louie piped up, "We gotta head back down." He was visibly antsy from the arduous ride and his long silence.

"Sorry we didn't see any bear or moose," the guide said as they hitched up their horses at trail's end.

"That's okay," she said. "I have a bear waiting for me in White Buffalo that I'm taking back to Ohio," she answered. She kissed Dollar on the nose.

"Right," the guide said, winking at her. She couldn't tell if he believed her or not.

THURSDAY, JULY 13TH

It was true. The bear was sitting on top of a suitcase next to the "For Sale" sign in front of Dutchie's trailer when they pulled up. An old woman with blue-black hair and wearing a purple caftan stood next to the bear.

"Dutchie's up in Kalispell. Trying to talk his way into fire-jumping one last time," she said. "He said you could stay here as long as you like. He'll be back in a week. Maybe." Both she and the bear were eating ice cream cones. Vanilla. Sammi couldn't decide which was more absurd: Dutchie trying to fire-jump or the bear eating a vanilla ice cream cone.

"Uh-huh. We gotta get back. I'm getting itchy," Uncle Louie told the old woman.

Sammi rented a Dodge minivan to take them and the bear back to Ohio. The bear sat politely in the back seat, wearing a Sony Walkman with extra large headphones and listening to Nadja Salerno-Sonnenberg play Brahms's *Violin Concerto in D* over and over again.

MID-JULY

Sammi drove the whole way. She got to know her Uncle Louie and how his brain and heart ticked, through the pastel layers of the Big Horn mountains. Twilight in the twisty Big Horns, the van just missed an enormous, free-ranging, black cow with astonishing skull-mask markings on its face. The bear turned and hooted at the cow, then said, "Whew," so distinctly, she and Louie laughed out loud. And as they pushed 95 mph all through Wyoming, Uncle Louie got her to understand the intrinsic comfort and confidence the Big House grants prisoners: "You know you're in Hell, but you're still standing. Breathing. Laughing. Even with that undercurrent simmering around the horrible men who did horrible things, threatening to boil over—it does boil over a lot—and still you gather for meals, prayer services, woodworking classes, and stuff. Yep. I *know* I can do Hell now. And that's a good and a bad place to be."

In Cody, Sammi stopped at a hair salon and asked to have her hair dyed blue-black. Zola, the Comanche stylist, refused, saying, "blue-black would age you even more." Instead, he cut her hair into a short-short Sassoon style and dyed it blonde with platinum and strawberry highlights.

"Now, you can say you've been scalped by a Comanche," Zola said and laughed wickedly.

"She bought a bear and then she got scalped," she said, laughing back.

BY THE WAY

Sammi had self-dissolved so much, she often spoke and even thought of herself in third person. *She ought to leave the bastard*, she'd think. Or, *She wants a cigarette.*

Looking back on the Lake Nippissing vacation, she thinks, *And that's when she became obsessed with bears.* As if her girlhood and even early adulthood memories are stories she read or heard about someone else, but not really hers. *And she studied French through school, until she became preoccupied with all things Russian—language, literature, history—in college. She used to brag about her extensive knowledge of the Cyrillic alphabet. But she kept her bear obsession a secret. What would she call herself: a Bear Buff? A Bare Buff? Ha Ha.*

HEAT WAVES AND SLEEPLESSNESS

In the rippling heat of the South Dakota flats and badlands she tired of Louie's talk of shivs, fisting, and crooked guards; she wanted to be alone with the bear. At Wall Drugs, she bought 70 pounds of raw rump roast and charged it on her Visa Platinum. She didn't bother filling the meat cooler with ice.

"Bobo will eat piles of maggots on months-old pork," Dutchie had told her. She remembered the admiration in Dutchie's voice when he said this and she, too, couldn't help but admire this about the bear. Even though she'd been vegetarian for more than two decades.

She had to toss the bear's scuffed, mustard-colored suitcase to make room for the cooler. She sorted through the bear's beaded vests, baggy satin shorts, armbands, paisley ties, and Shriner's hats, and found a bleary Polaroid snapshot stuck awkwardly in a frame too big for it. In the snapshot, Dutchie and the bear were locked in a tight hug, and wore matching multicolored sequined vests and fezzes topped with purple tassels. Dutchie beamed into the camera and she would swear the bear was smiling, too. She kept the snapshot, but dumped the suitcase and its contents in a garbage barrel when they stopped at the Badlands Information Center. She also kept the bear-sized leather Stetson with under-the-chin straps. The bear favored it.

Near Sioux City, the bear became agitated by the smell of meat-rendering plants. Uncle Louie got jumpy, too. "Let me off here," he told her. "A friend of a friend here has a line on some OxyContin. Good luck to you, sweetheart."

She dropped Uncle Louie off at Jimbo's SuperDrugs after buying boxes of candy bars and magazines for Bear to flip through on the way back.

To keep his mind off the stench of the Midwest. The fetid stink of Ohio's banal busyness and soul-grinding industry was already evident all the way in Iowa.

He moaned once, Bear, at a stoplight on the edge of Illinois, and thumped the top of his paw down on a page in *Redbook*. It was a glossy ad: a vampish cartoon woman with a Clara Bow bob, deep décolletage, and a sapphire—the same brilliant blue of her shimmy dress—sparkling from the middle of her forehead. The vamp was holding a cigarette. A Camel Select.

Sammi stopped at the next gas station and bought a pack of Camels, no filters. She lit one and tried to get Bear to take it. Nothing doing. She tried to place it between his lips. What he had of lips. No. He was all patience with her spreading apart the folds of his muzzle, gently, gingerly, with her fingers, but he would not clamp down on the cigarette. Frustrated, she smoked the cigarette herself, in the front seat with the van running and the air-conditioner on.

"Hey, lady, " a bone-thin, red-haired trucker rapped at her window. "That a bear in there?"

"Yes," she said, and drove off.

By the time she got back to the mud-thick humidity of Ohio, she was smoking a Camel, no filter, every hour.

"Driving you on these highways, through this country, this is great, wickedly brave. Good, strong. My greatest accomplishment," she told Bear. She was exhausted. Hadn't slept in days, just kept driving, and her hands shook from the endless coffee and cigarettes. She caught herself, more than once, wondering if Bear could drive and if she should ask him to take over the wheel. "Greater than . . . greater than . . . greater than pushing Madeline through my crotch with no meds at all," she finally came up with.

Maddie, her only child, was attending MIT on scholarship. Maddie—her greatest joy, her pride, her crowning, crowing achievement—at college now tinkering with technology and sex and who knows what else? How can driving a wild beast across America be greater than bearing, laboring, and raising a good child?

SHE'S BACK

"I'm back," she yelled toward Paul, who was sitting, as usual, in his home office in front of his computer. From 8 A.M. until 5 P.M. it was computer programming and "visiting clients." From 6 until 9, it was computer gaming. From 9 until—*who knew*—it was computer pornography.

"What? No postcard? No cowgirl boots? No souvenirs?" he shouted.

"Yes. I've brought a bear," she said.

"Whatever," Paul answered.

Sammi called Maddie at MIT.

"Everything all right, Mom? Did ya have a good trip? Dad still there?"

"Yes," she said. "I've brought back a bear to live with me."

"Yeah, right. Whatever," Maddie said. "Well, I got my tongue pierced."

"What?" Sammi asked. "Why?"

"Makes it more fun for the man. You *know*," Maddie giggled.

Sammi thought a minute. "Click it on the phone so I can believe you."

A sigh. Another giggle. Then a faint, tinny "clickclickclick." The kiss of billiard balls. Frail braces sparking off braces on a frantically hot first date. Then the click of Maddie's cell shutting off.

Sammi's cats left home. She caught glimpses of them in odd corners of the neighborhood every once in a while, but they never returned to be fed. Stella, her true-hearted German shepherd, held her ground, growling the lowest grumble she could muster without making it a threat.

"Yes, Stella, you were my first sable bear," she told her dog. "My bristle-haired, bear-hug girl. Now, we have a real bear."

She set Bear up in the guest room. He liked the old quilts, the queen-sized, green iron bed with ornate ball finials on each of the four posts. He spent hours unscrewing and then re-screwing those four finial balls into the four posts. He enjoyed wearing the oversized gorilla slippers she bought him off the Internet. He savored the ready-made salads *sans* dressing and the raw round-tip steaks she fed him three or four times a day. He loved watching *Absolutely Fabulous* re-runs on TV: he grunted happily every time Pats lit a cigarette.

He let her brush his teeth every morning and every night.

She spent most of her day feeding Bear and watching his old bicycle tricks in the driveway. He rode Maddie's old pink Barbie bicycle Sammi pulled from the cluttered garage and he wore his gorilla slippers while he biked.

"Is that a bear in your driveway?" the neighbors asked.

"Yes."

"Are you allowed to do that?"

"Yes."

Sammi worked out a wholesale deal with Frankie, the Sicilian down at Joe's Fishhouse. Frankie liked Bear, but couldn't allow him into the store.

In fact, she had a very hard time finding places that welcomed Bear anywhere near them.

"Is that a bear, lady?" the police officer asked her in the park, where Bear was giddily biking, pedaling fast, and then taking his feet off the pedals to glide with his legs up in the air.

"Yes," she said.

"Don't think you're allowed to bring him here."

"Yes, I think I am. He's trained."

Several tickets later, she discovered that NO, she didn't need a license to have a bear, but Bear wasn't welcome in any public place.

THE SPIFFY SWIFTY GAS STATION

Dante Mourning, the young black man with a full 60's fro who ran the gas station, was the first to welcome Bear. She'd always liked this young man. She loved his fro. It was rebellion against a world that no longer cared to notice rebellion. Whenever she paid for her gas, Dante smiled so warm and happy to see her, as if he'd been waiting for her the whole day; well, who wouldn't fall in love with this young man? Sometimes, she'd admit to herself that if she were just a bit younger, and decided to go the young-lover route, he would be the one she'd seduce.

"Jesus H. Christ, that a bear in your car?" he asked her.

"Yes."

"Can I see him?"

"Yes."

"Man, bring him in here."

"You sure?"

"Yeah, man. I got a cousin in the circus. The Motor City Ragtag Zoo and Traveling Show. You ever hear of it?"

"Yes," she lied.

"My cousin Jones knows about bears. Would lose his shit about this, man. Make him so freaking happy."

She handed Bear out of the backseat and pulled his bicycle from the trunk of the car. Bear rode in gleeful circles under the neon of the late-night gas station. Neon like circus spotlights.

"I love that bear, man. Bring him back."

Bear loved the gas station lights and wide concrete and the handsome young man.

"Yes. I will."

She showered Bear daily in the double-wide, double rainshower-headed, Italian-tiled shower she and Paul had designed the years they believed that having a perfect house, perfect rooms, perfect bathroom fixtures would bring them perfect happiness. She wore her bathing suit and got in with Bear, scrubbing him with a horse brush. He hummed and hooted when she rubbed the brush up and down his back and rump.

She bought Bear mint-flavored dental floss and he sat pretty every night while she cleaned his teeth. She used the floss, too, after secretly smoking Camel Selects late into the night in her backyard. She imagined the wind blowing over her was wind that had danced over the mountains and plains of Montana and into her backyard just to rattle her trees. The same wind that knocked against Dutchie's trailer the hours he prattled his way through Bear's history. Sometimes, the wind mimicked a horse's whinny.

Bear sat in the lounge chair next to her as she smoked, listening to Moby, The Strokes, Tom Waits, or Prokofiev on the iPod she'd bought him. The volume was so loud, she heard echoes from his earbuds. Bear always tapped his claws on the armrests during Waits's "Goin' out West." They relaxed, but she also worried, trying to puzzle out other places where she could take Bear.

Our Lady of Sorrow, the Catholic Church she said was their family parish and hadn't attended in years, would not allow Bear. Not even if he wore the strong yet stylish harness she'd fashioned for him out of wide elastic covered with purple velvet. "Who on earth wants to bring a bear to church? He's a beast, a brute; he's no sense of morals, no real soul," she overheard the organist tell the priest.

"Fiends, hypocrites," Sammi whispered. She withdrew their parish card.

Carol Stone, her next-door neighbor, suggested her United Faith Church on Broad Street. "They accept everybody," Carol told her. Carol had spent the previous year traveling in Nepal, India, Ireland, Wales, Egypt. . . . Well, she really put some miles on her soles and had self-realized that she was a macrobiotic pagan celibate, had divorced her husband Jack, and was using the alimony to support her new church.

The Broad Street church did accept Bear, and they sat in the front row of United Faith every Sunday the rest of that summer. The church invited her and Bear to their Drag Queen Bingo events, to benefit the AIDS Foundation. Bear rode his bicycle, much to the Bingo-ers' delight, during intermission, after Trixie's Judy Garland Tribute.

Forget your troubles, come on, get happy . . .

THEN, LATE AUGUST CAME

"What the fuck are you doing with that bear?" Cindy asked at the annual neighborhood cookout.

"Why are you driving that fucking Hummer?" Sammi responded. "That gas-guzzling lakefront cabin on wheels."

"What?" Cindy looked genuinely confused. But then Cindy always did. "I feel *safe* in that thing. Don't knock it 'til you try it. I could drive that thing through Hell without a scratch." Cindy was into her fifth gin and tonic. Gin drinkers always take themselves too seriously.

Sammi was on her third Seven-and-Seven. Whiskey drinkers can get mean. "Cindy, Cindy, Cindy, let me tell you something. When you sit out in the backyard at night, the Montana wind blowing over you . . . cigarettes glowing . . . whiskey pouring . . . the moon staring down at you . . . and a bear sitting right next to you, you know damn well that *nothing* could be more dangerous than a loose bear. But you sit there knowing it and knowing that you're surviving it. And I *know* now that I can live through Hell. And that's a good and a bad place to be."

Cindy continued to look confused. But she did hand Sammi a keeper, "You're drunk. You're speechifying."

Sammi laughed until she snorted. She liked the word "speechifying" a lot. Especially after having whiskey. She laughed so hard, Cindy started laughing, too. Their laughter meant they couldn't walk away mad at each other, as they usually did, so they returned to convivial cattiness.

"You hear that Constance O'Donnel's fertility treatments finally worked? Yep. Knocked up with a boy. Due in January. Her own son is going to be younger than her two grandsons."

"How much did that cost?"

"One-hundred and fifty thousand."

Sammi whistled. "That would pay for a pretty piece of Wyoming."

Later that night, the iPod's power pack tanked. She dragged out a dusty cassette player from the garage and put Nat King Cole in when she and Bear went outdoors for cigarettes and to soak up the night.

As soon as Nat began crooning "It's Only a Paper Moon," Bear rose from his lounge chair and began swaying his hips and shoulders to the music.

> *Say, it's only a paper moon*
> *Sailing over a cardboard sea*
> *But it wouldn't be make-believe*
> *If you believed in me . . .*

Bear's head tilted and he held his arms around an imaginary partner. One of the tricks Dutchie had forgotten to tell her about, she guessed. She slipped her right hand into Bear's left paw and her left hand around his fat, hairy, substantially real waist.

The pads of his paws were surprisingly soft and pliable, like human hands. A circus bear, he'd never suffered the scratches, gashes, and calluses that digging into rocks and gravel, or ripping through bark inevitably bring.

All summer, she'd let him shovel around for grubs and insects and now their ChemGreen lawn was pocked with shallow holes and small mounds of shredded sod. Still, his filed nails were clean and manicured enough for polish.

They danced. He lifted her off the ground so her heart beat next to his heart. Their heartbeats synchronized like the wings of a heron flock and their hips gyrated and swayed perfectly in time, like they were rewinding the clock of the Universe. They danced under the blank white eye of the moon—her feet not touching the ground—even after the tape snapped off.

His snout came close and she rubbed the velvet of his ears and the soft slope between his eyes. The dark of his eyes like muddy rivers rushing into springtime. His eyes held hers. She swam in his eyes and his sway until she knew she'd better let go or she would never let go.

He had no lips to kiss. So she lifted the pad of his left paw and kissed it gently three times. She did the same with his right paw and then she placed it on her breast, held it over her heart briefly.

And then Bear continued to dance and twirl. He held up his muzzle and arms to the spotlight of moon.

AN OBLIQUE REDEMPTION

Dante seemed to be waiting, alone, smiling.

"Sugar," she said. "I've got to put this Bear somewhere else for awhile."

"Sister, gas is getting too high. People getting crabbier and crabbier. And the world's ending soon. What the hell? Whatever. I've got to move on. Do something better these last days," Dante said. "I talked to Jones and he wants me to join his show. How much you want for Bear?"

"Take him."

"You're shittin' me. You love that Bear."

"Yes." She thought of how she loved Bear. She thought of how many times Bear had made her say "Yes." More times than ever. How Bear hadn't been wild for long enough and how maybe she could do some wild living for him. She thought of going back to where   bear and wind and wildness came from—gusts and hats and horses.

"No cruelty?" Sammi asked.

"Cross my heart and bless my soul," Dante placed her hand over his heart. His eyes were brown spring rivers, like Bear's.

"Then, yes."

A SPONTANEOUSLY PLANNED RETURN

September was whispering its way into fall. The mountain roads would be impassable soon with snow—snow that had to be seen to be believed. She knew she had to leave now. She could get herself back to Dutchie's trailer and fill Thunder's barn again. She could buy a horse. She knew she could learn to brush and floss a horse's teeth. File his hooves. *I know I can ride like the Devil*, Sammi said to herself.

The Finalists

Animal Control 🐝

JACOB M. APPEL

Some small towns in New England still elect their dog catchers, but down here animal control has always been a civil service post. You log forty hours of coursework in chemical immobilization and euthanasia, pass a multiple choice exam, write out a check for eighty-five dollars payable to the Virginia Department of Agriculture—and before you can say sweet Jesus on a flapjack, you've got a job you can't lose, short of sticking your pecker in a rabid groundhog. But that doesn't mean it's all country ham and gravy. Not hardly. You don't know stress until you've told the parents of a nine year old kid that you're going to put down his beloved Lassie or Old Yeller. Which is why, when the field supervisor pokes his head into the dayroom, I get a wallop of those cat-on-a-hot-roof jitters. There's just me and Josie today—Lisa May's out on her honeymoon in Las Vegas—so I know some unlucky critter somewhere has my number.

It's nearly noon and I'm reading a book about hoaxes. My sister-in-law's recommendation. Josie is cooking up catfish in a pan. The dayroom smells like frying.

"Ready to earn your bread, Mr. Dipple?" asks the field manager. He's not a bad egg, as bosses go, but he's third-generation veterinarian, so he thinks he's just a speck better than everybody else. He insists on calling us Mr. Dipple, and Miss Jackson, and Miss Bickmore—though I guess Miss Bickmore's going to be Mrs. Butts from now on—and we're supposed to call him Dr. Molinary, at least to his face. As if we work in a grammar school or a post office. What takes the cake about Doc Molinary is he wears cream-colored suits, like Errol Flynn, even in winter. "I have police already on the scene," he says. "County patrol on their way."

"Let me guess. Another stolen monkey." We've got a big research hospital in Spotsylvania County now—and last year a gang of animal liberation folks attempted to spring free a chimpanzee. Damn monkey went bonkers.

We spent nearly six hours trying to coax it down from the ferris wheel at the fairgrounds. "If I buy another thousand bananas at that Winn-Dixie, the manager will have me committed."

"No monkey business, I'm afraid," says Molinary. "Try a tiger."

I look at my watch. April 1st is still two days away. "A tiger?"

"On the loose in Hollow Grove. Escaped from an outfit licensed in North Carolina. The Forepaugh Family Traveling Circus." He hands me the manila folder that contains the intake sheet. "You'd better hurry. It's seems our tiger has already made away with an eight month old baby."

Josie flips off the gas range. "So much for lunch," she says.

"Good luck, Mr. Dipple. Good luck, Miss Jackson," says the field manager, a bit too formal—like some Old West mayor sending John Wayne to fight bandits. "You go after the tiger. I'll handle the reporters. We'll see who comes back alive."

Doc Molinary smiles, pleased with his own joke. I smile back. I don't bother to tell him that his fly is unzipped.

❧

It's a gorgeous day, probably over seventy. Makes you think those Global Warming people know what they're talking about. The birch trees along Princess Anne Street have started to leaf. Robins are feeding in front of the Washington Mutual. Young mothers crowd the walkways beside the Rappahannock. It's hard to remember that, a century before I was born, General Burnside lost twelve thousand men trying to take this ground from Lee's Virginians. Don't get me wrong: I'm not some wacko with a Confederate battle flag on his bumper. I've got nothing personal against people moving out here from Washington or Alexandria. Everybody has to live somewhere. I just think it's important a guy know what happened in a place before he showed up.

I adjust the rearview mirror and ease the van into traffic. It feels odd to be driving with the sirens. "There used to be these giant elm trees all along here," I say to Josie.

"I'm sure there were. Good, sturdy lynching trees," says Josie. She's only in her late-twenties, but she's the first black animal control officer in Virginia. Her fiancé teaches criminal justice at Mary Washington. "Say, you're the movie buff. Isn't there an old movie about a tiger on the loose? Something with Gregory Peck?"

It's true. I do watch a lot of movies. My marriage to Gwen is like that.

"*Bringing Up Baby*," I say. "Katharine Hepburn keeps it for a pet. But it's Cary Grant, not Gregory Peck. And it's a leopard, not a tiger."

"Well, pardon me for living," says Josie, grinning.

"On the subject of tigers, you got a location in Hollow Grove?"

Josie reads me an address from the folder. She must sense something in my reaction, because she asks, "You familiar with the place?"

I know the Minard place, all right. I grew up out in Hollow Grove— back when it was the only subdivision between D.C. and Richmond. All that land had once been Minard land. Years later, when I was at Virginia State, I took a class in Southern history, and the professor, who had this thing against suburbs, kept calling Hollow Grove "Levittown for crackers." That's total bullshit, of course. My papa taught accounting at a private high school and my mama did social work for the county. But there's no point explaining things to people who don't want to know them.

"I *used to* be familiar with the place. Before you were born," I tell Josie. "Screwy family lived out there, but I'm sure they're all gone now." I take the Hollow Grove exit off the turnpike and cross the railroad tracks onto Culpepper Avenue. "Fact is, I'm surprised the old place is still standing."

Or maybe it's not still standing, I realize. The same address doesn't have to mean the same building. It could be a Chevy dealership these days. Or a porno theater. That's why I never drive out here. If I had kids, maybe I'd want to show off my old stomping grounds. Who knows? But I don't have kids.

It turns out the entire subdivision is gone. Ploughed over by the new interstate to Charlottesville. There's a motel where my house stood. It's got a Dutch theme. Windmill over the office. Tulips and daffodils out front. That's one thing we never have a shortage of in this lifetime. Bad ideas. I don't tell Josie I used to live here.

Then we turn up Lady Randolph Street—and it's the same house. An old colonial with two chimneys. There's about six gazillion squad cars out front—state police, Spotsylvania County, Prince George County, Fredericksburg traffic enforcement—not to mention enough fire trucks for an Independence Day parade. The television crews have set up shop on the other side of a sawhorse cordon. I'm not even out of the van when the commander on-scene, this huge bald guy with a walrus mustache, is practically up my nose. "You animal control?" he demands.

"That's what it says on the van," I say.

"It's about time," he says. "This one takes the cake. I got an escaped tiger snatching a baby off the back porch and carrying it up a beech tree."

"It is injured?"

"Hard to say. You can't see much with all those the evergreens. It was crying for a while, for what it's worth, but now it's stopped."

I shake my head. "Not the kid. The tiger."

"Oh, the tiger," says the commander. "How the hell should I know?"

"Well, let's go have a look," I say.

Josie hands me the tranquilizer gun and we start up the steep driveway.

That's when I see her. She's much thinner today, you could even say too thin, but she still carries herself like a fat girl. Her hair is gray as steel wool. It matches her sweater. You can tell she's been crying, but now she's got this totally blank look and she's rocking back and forth like some sort of Bible-thumper. Her husband isn't half bad looking. A few years younger than she is, not too short—only his face is a bit blotchy. He's got his arm around Evangelina's shoulder.

I steel myself and walk directly up to her.

"Good morning, Miss Minard," I say.

She looks puzzled. "Mrs. Stevens, now," she says. "Do I know you?"

Not a hint of recognition. But I guess she has other things on her mind.

"Animal control," is what I answer. "Tell me what happened."

This might be a good point to mention that I wasn't a popular teenager. I didn't cut it as an athlete, I certainly was no rocket scientist in the classroom, and it didn't help any to be the son of Melvin Dipple, who taught bookkeeping with a pencil over his ear and chalk-prints on the seat of his trousers. My brother compensated for his shortcomings with humor—and he won permanent social acceptance after he filled the deputy headmaster's Oldsmobile Tornado with six thousand nickel-plated ball bearings. I tried to follow in Albert's footsteps, but I just wasn't funny. By eleventh grade, I threw in the towel on cool. Instead, I took up birdwatching.

While Carter and Reagan bickered over leading the Free World, I went thrashing through the underbrush for woodpeckers and wrens. I wore a mesh pith helmet that my brother bought for a summer-stock production of *Lawrence of Arabia*. The hat came with a leather chin strap and a veil of mosquito netting. I also had a pair of Zeiss field glasses my Grandpa Cavanaugh brought back from North Africa. He was an artillery officer during the war. Probably the only Dipple or Cavanaugh ever to do anything important. For camouflage, I spread guacamole on my cheeks.

My goal was to spot all eight hundred species in the Peterson guide. Not that I cared so much about birds. What I wanted was accomplishment. Fossils or model horses would have done as well. But having picked birds, I hunted them with a vengeance.

Mostly, I kept to the subdivision. Sometimes I crosses the high meadow and ducked under the split-rail fence into the Minard's enormous backyard. The overgrown tea roses were great for hummingbirds, except when the hounds were outside. And the Minard's property was like a hidden amusement park. Some of the money from the farmland had gone into a private playground. A swingset. Monkey bars. A heart-shaped sandbox. They also had clay tennis courts, but they didn't maintain them. Being in the Minard yard never felt like trespassing, but I didn't dare ride on the swings. And then one evening—a long twilight in early spring—I was watching two large black birds perched atop the Minard's weathervane when Mr. Minard snuck up behind me.

Mr. Minard was tall and slender with a baby face, but in his forties he already walked with a stoop, and his skin was the color of cucumber pulp. I knew all about the man without ever having met him. If you lived in Hollow Grove, this was what you talked about. Darwin Minard had been raised by his mama—up north—then came back to the homestead with an overweight wife and the ugliest baby anybody could remember. The wife had sung opera once, but had a tumor on her voice box.

Mr. Minard dabbed his forehead with his handkerchief—as though encountering me was a cause of considerable exertion. "See anything interesting?" he asked.

"Ravens," I said defensively.

"Hmmm. Look like crows to me."

Mr. Minard broke off a sprig of forsythia and sniffed it approvingly. "How do you know they're not crows?" he asked.

They *were* crows, of course. We both knew that. But I also realized he thought I was a peeping Tom, which I wasn't.

"They're too large for crows," I said. "Their beaks are too thick."

He nodded. "Ravens. How do you like that?"

Mr. Minard snapped off several more sprays of forsythia and tucked them into a wet dish towel. He was assembling a bouquet.

"You think she's pretty, don't you?" he asked.

"Who's pretty?"

But just then I caught sight of Evangelina Minard standing at one of the dormer windows under the weathervane. She was the year behind me in school. Walleyed. Fat as a Turk. In the habit of fanning her neck with her hands. There was a limerick about Evangelina and a suckling pig graffitied in one of the boys' bathrooms.

Mr. Minard reached into his pants pocket and toyed with his keys.

"What's your name?" he asked.

I considered a secret identity. All I could think of were Clark Kent and Peter Parker. "Jethro Dipple," I said.

"Well, Jethro Dipple," he said, "When I was your age, I used to hide in the *au pair*'s closet. Fjola from Iceland. *Fj-o-la*. She was probably about twenty-five years old—and she would strip down in front of the mirror to look at herself. One day, I sneezed and she caught me—and I was positive she was going to tell my mother, but she didn't. For the rest of that summer, she let me sit on the bed while I watched."

"I should go home now," I said.

"No need for that," he said. "You're missing the whole point of my story."

"I wasn't doing anything," I said.

"I tell you what," said Mr. Minard. "Why don't you stay for supper? I'm sure Evangelina would be delighted."

I tried to object. Being un-cool was one thing. Being known as the guy who spied on Evangelina Minard was another. But what could I do? You don't have leverage when you're sixteen and covered in avocado dip. Either I followed Evangeline's father up to the big house, or I made a chancy dash through the brush. I searched for a break in the azalea hedge—but deep down I was a coward. Soon enough, I found myself standing in the Minard's big country kitchen.

The room's walls were large square timbers. All except around the hearth, which was exposed yellow brick. Assorted pots hung from the rafters. Silver candlesticks sat on the walnut dinner table. But there was also a modern oven, a dishwasher, and a double-doored Kelvinator refrigerator. The oven stood open, and a servant girl with an enormous rump was bent over it, rotating a turkey. Mrs. Minard hovered nearby, sipping a vermillion cocktail. She was big, but with shorts legs. Like a cartoon ox. Not un-pretty, just fat. Mr. Minard said I'd come to have dinner with Evangeline.

"Does he have a name?" asked Mrs. Minard, her voice like sandpaper.

They both looked at me. "Jethro Dipple," I said.

"Dipple. I know Dipple," she said. "He's the one with the tiny little balls."

She meant the ball bearings. "That's my brother," I said.

"It seems like we're being inundated by Dipples," said Mrs. Minard—and she laughed fiercely. "No matter. I think it's about time Evangelina had a boyfriend."

As though on cue, the daughter walked into the kitchen. She was chewing gum.

"There you are, darling," said Mrs. Minard. "I was telling your friend here that you could use a boyfriend."

This was the only time—for a split second—that I felt bad for Evangelina Minard. Because we were *not* friends. We'd never exchanged two words in our lives. And we weren't going to be friends. Or I felt bad because the idea of her having a boyfriend—*ever*—seemed so totally impossible. The poor girl gasped when she saw me. She looked as though she'd just dropped a baby. "Oh my God," she said.

"Jethro here has been attempting to spy on you," said Mr. Minard.

I hid the field glasses behind my folded arms. Shame burned the tips of my ears.

"Gross," exclaimed Evangelina.

"You should be flattered," said Mr. Minard. "I told you it was only a matter of time before you turned into a swan."

This made Evangelina blush. "Daddy!"

"I have an idea," said Mrs. Minard. "Darling, we still have some time before supper is ready. Why don't you model for your friend here?" The woman turned to me and added: "Evangelina is going to be a great stage actress someday. She's very talented. All she needs to do is reduce a bit."

"Please, Mommy," said Evangelina. "I don't want to."

"It will be fun," said Mrs. Minard. "And good experience. Especially with company."

I looked to the servant for help, but the girl was painting butter on the turkey as though nothing were out of the ordinary. If Evangelina's father had turned me in for peeping, I could have lived with that. Somehow. But going from peeper to "company" was downright freaky. Evangelina must have thought so too. Her small dark eyes had taken on a watery, desperate look.

"Let's ask the boy," said her mother. "Jethro, wouldn't you like Evangelina to model for you?"

It crossed my mind that she might mean *naked* modeling. Or at least lingerie. In that house, anything was possible. "I guess so," I said. When I was sixteen, even Evangelina Minard was worth seeing in the nude.

My imagination quickly got the better of me. I was dreaming of bikinis, silk garters, kimonos from Japan. Evangelina Minard casually stepping out of peignoirs in front of floor-to-ceiling mirrors. But my fantasies quickly came down crashing. The daughter disappeared through the kitchen door and returned an eternity later wearing a smock-like maroon evening gown a good forty years out of style. She had a string of black pearls around her neck and a hideous costume brooch pinned to her chest. The brooch was jade green and shaped like a moth. Evangeline posed with

her plump hand on her equally plump hip. She had trouble balancing herself on her five-inch heels. Meanwhile, I tried to wipe off the guacamole
with my sleeve.

"My grand-aunt left us a whole steamer trunk of winter dresses," said
Mrs. Minard. That explained the sudden, pungent odor of naphthalene. "My
grand-aunt was a Delacroix from Savannah."

"Isn't she stunning?" asked Mr. Minard. "Who do you think she looks
more like—Marlene Dietrich or Greta Garbo?"

"You're showing your age, dearest," answered his wife. "I'm sure he's
never hear of either of them. Try Farrah Fawcett or Raquel Welch."

It struck me that both of the adult Minards might be drunk. Mrs.
Minard did indeed pour herself another cocktail. "Why don't you show us
something décolleté, darling?" she urged her daughter "Maybe the lilac chiffon?" And Evangelina dutifully tottered out of the room.

"I tell you, Jethro Dipple, some young man out there is going to be very
lucky one of these days," said Mr. Minard. "He's going to win the heart of a
spectacular girl." I instantly thought of winning a piñata at the Mexican raf-
fle. "And I don't mind saying, he's also going to find himself in an extremely
advantageous position financially."

That's when I realized he knew the truth. They both knew. That their
daughter was hideous as sin. Somehow, that made the fashion show even
less bearable. I nearly bowled over the servant girl on my race toward the
rear steps.

I can't imagine Evangelina's reaction when she showed up in her lilac
chiffon evening gown—and her audience was gone. But she couldn't have
been none too happy. By the following afternoon, the entire school knew
I'd been spying on her.

So here I am. Face to face with the girl who ruined me in high school.
And also the lucky guy who finally won the piñata. In the same overgrown
yard where I was once afraid to climb on the monkey bars. But everything's
totally different now, of course. Because twenty-five years have gone by, and

they've got a baby up a tree, and I'm packing the only tranquilizer gun in miles. Fate can have a mean sense of humor.

I wait patiently while Evangelina tells me about the tiger. "I was inside hardly half a minute," she says. "Just taking Daddy's breakfast up to his room. I saw it through the upstairs window."

"You live with your father, Mrs. Stevens?" I ask.

Evangelina nods. She is sobbing again. Her husband adds: "She takes care of him. He's not right anymore, you understand."

So the old man's gone off the deep end. I can't help taking some pleasure in this.

"Do you think there's a chance . . . ?" Mr. Stevens lets his sentence trail away.

"We'll do our best," I say. "We always do." I'm not sure why I add this second part—maybe I don't want him to think we're cooking up anything special.

I turn away abruptly and follow the commander out to the tree. Josie is on her cell phone, discussing big cats with the Capital Zoo. We've also been joined by a ruddy, muscular guy in his seventies, a real Jack LaLanne type, who keeps the animals for the Forepaugh family. His name is Ted Serspinski. His wardrobe staples are panama hat, alligator boots, and bola tie. "The darnedest thing," he says, not too fazed. "But I suppose that's what we have insurance for." He has mentioned the welfare of the tiger, Duchess, half a dozen times. He hasn't said a word about the baby.

We stop under the tree. It's in a thicket of cedars, so you can't see very far up. Occasionally, there's a flurry of branches. "You're wrong," I tell the commander. "It's not a beech tree. It's a basswood."

"You fucking kidding?" asks the commander. "You a fucking botanist or something?"

I stay deadpan. "I wouldn't kid you. It's definitely a basswood."

The commander doesn't know what to make of this. He's resting one hand on the handle of his billy club and the other on his service revolver. But I guess he thinks I'm a wackjob—and there's no sense arguing with a wackjob. "If it's a basswood, it's a basswood," he says. "You think you can shoot the damn thing from down here?"

I balance the tranquilizer gun on my shoulder and aim into the greenery. "Not a chance in hell," I say. "Maybe I can get a better angle from the roof of the house."

The circus guy doesn't like this idea. "You can't be serious," he objects. "She could fall out of the tree."

"Goddammit," says the commander. "If you get a shot, shoot."

"Are you sure about that?" I ask. "He might have a point. What if it knocks the kid out of the tree on the way down?"

The commander looks at me like I killed his dog. "Goddamit," he says again.

I turn to Josie. "Any ideas?"

"Actually, I do," she says. "According to Washington, we shouldn't do anything. If it hasn't harmed the kid yet, it's not going to. We should just sit on our hands until it decides it's ready to come down."

The commander spits into the dust. "So we're just supposed to wait for it to make the first move?"

"That looks like the plan," I say.

"They're going to send out their cat-keeper, but it may take a while," says Josie. "He's on jury duty and they've got to track him down."

That just takes the cake. Jury duty. Another lucky break for the Minards.

I send Josie back to the truck for my camping chair. Then I cozy up with my sister-in-law's book: *DUPED: The 100 Greatest Deceptions of All Time*. But it's hard to focus. I keep thinking about Evangelina, and about meeting her like this, and about how everything turned out. She's obviously not a great stage actress. And I'm not some expert on big cats who gets called in from D.C. I'm not even a vet or a cop. I'm just some civil service lackey with a dietician wife and no kids who knows a helluva lot about black and white movies. All in all, we're both rather damn ordinary. Which is pretty okay, I suppose, once you get used to it. But sometimes you can't help wondering how things might be different: If I'd been popular in high school. If I'd married Evangelina Minard. If Gwen hadn't had a hysterectomy. I fold the hoax book on my chest and lean back for a one-eyed nap.

At some point, a uniformed cop shows up with a bag of sandwiches. Somebody must have gotten his orders crossed, because another cop appears ten seconds later with two pizzas and a case of Dr. Pepper. It feels kind of strange to be chowing down while there's an escaped tiger in the tree above you—but that's what public service is like. You do what you can do. And sometimes you do what you can't do. In between, you stop for a pastrami on rye bread.

"You want to hear something amazing?" I ask the circus guy.

"What's that?"

"In England back in the '50s, they showed a television special on the spaghetti harvest in Italy. It was part of an April Fool's Day hoax. And people bought it—hook, line and sinker."

"Is that so?"

"They got letters from people asking where they could buy spaghetti trees."

I can tell the guy doesn't give two slaps about hoaxes. Probably has no idea he's standing half a mile from Stonewall Jackson's HQ. Or that in my twelfth grade, Duke Crenshaw passed around a petition to change the Virginia state bird to the "Peeping Dipple." Why should he want to know about me? All the circus guy cares about is his cats. And all Evangelina cares about is her baby. And all Doc Molinary cares about is keeping his first name out of the public record. We're a bunch of screw-ups, aren't we? People, I mean.

"You want another sandwich?" I ask circus guy. "We've got bologna, corned beef . . . and this one looks like bologna and turkey."

That's when the commotion erupts behind us. It's Evangelina's husband. The cops are trying to restrain him, but he won't back off.

"Let the guy through," I say.

The commander glares at me. "Let him through," he says.

Stevens comes directly to me. He must think I'm in charge. The guy must have come straight from the office—he's still wearing his tie and a tweed jacket with elbow pads. The tie has these tiny white anchors on it.

"What's up?" I ask.

"We've been waiting and waiting and waiting. This is killing us," he says, short of breath. "Can't you do something already."

The circus guy is standing next to me. "We've got to wait her down. It's the safest for both of them."

Stevens goes up like someone's lit a firecracker in his ass. "Both of them!" he shouts. "That's my goddamn son in that tree. If you don't do something—right goddamn now—I swear I'm going to do something myself."

The commander warns him to calm down. Like that does any good. Nothing to relax a panicked dad like a cop flexing muscle.

"You want us to do something," I say. "Okay, we'll do something."

"What about waiting?" demands circus guy.

"You heard the man. He wants action," I answer. "Anyone know how to get one of those machines they use on utility poles? You know what I mean. . . . Apple pickers?"

"Cherry pickers," says Josie.

"That's right," I say. "Get me one of those. Fast."

I've never ridden in one of these things before. For ordinary house pets, we go up in a ladder. Not glamorous, but it does the job. And it's cheap. Cherry pickers, on the other hand, are a once-in-a-lifetime opportunity, so I'm set on making the most of this.

At first, the guy down below does all of the steering. He pulls his levers and I'm up at the first branches, then higher than the Minard's roof. But it's me who has to direct the final few yards. "Left," I call out. "Up. Left. More left." The basket of the cherry picker snaps cedar branches as it moves. "Stop," I command. "Right there."

"Can you see it?" Josie shouts.

I can see it, all right. The tiger's just lying there, on a thick basswood limb. Minding its own damn business. And the baby's just lying there too. In a fork between branches. Eyes closed. Scratch marks on its bare chest—but tree scratches, not claw marks. The child is quiet as a gravestone, but he's still breathing. I raise the tranquilizer gun to my shoulder. At first, I take aim at the tiger. But then it strikes me that I could just as easily hit the baby. Get back at Evangelina for twelfth grade. Take a little bit of the random power in the world for myself. Mistakes do happen. Otherwise, I've got a clean record. Who'd ever know the difference?

I focus on the baby, then the cat, then the baby. Beyond them, through a break in the cedars, I can see all of Fredericksburg: the glistening Rappahannock coiling its way toward the horizon, the bell tower of Mary Washington's, the churches and tobacco warehouses and the strip malls spreading south toward Richmond. My wife's out there too, probably watching this on the TV in the nurse's station. Below me, Josie and the circus guy and Evangelina's husband are all shading their eyes against the sun. I guess this is what it means to have your life flash before your eyes.

"You alright up there?" calls Josie.

"I'm fine," I shout back. "Give me a second."

And then I fire. Straight into the cat's shank. The animal jolts upright—and then crumples, crashing through the thicket below.

I hear screaming at ground level. The circus guy cursing. The commander ordering people to back off. Evangelina wailing, "My baby! My baby!" I pull the cherry picker toward the branch and scoop up the kid in my arms.

I'm still not sure I made the right call. Truth is, I'm still not sure a baby's worth more alive than a tiger. But it's not my job to figure that out. No point in asking questions about what's fair and what's right. No point at all. Because the danger is you'll start answering them. And that's great if you're the president or something, but not so good if you're an ordinary guy. I know where I'll end up if I start asking questions like that, and answering them, and it's no place I ever want to be.

Carker 🦌

MIRIAM GERSHOW

C ONFERENCES WENT SOMETHING LIKE THIS: JONNA WOULD WAIT IN THE front of her empty classroom, shifting from foot to foot like a show pony, resenting her dress suit. The wool would be pilly and too warm, the color an improbable green, having been bought on the suggestion of a wide-hipped, yeasty colleague. *A suit,* Mrs. Ostrem had stage-whispered in the teacher's lounge, *will age you a little. Parents like teachers with some life behind them.* Mrs. Ostrem had been teaching social studies at Brookswood High for nineteen years, and her breath was sour with coffee, her hair falling out of her bun in long, thick strands, as if she'd just been shaken too hard.

Jonna would check the back of the suit regularly for chalk marks. She would try not to lean against her board. She would look out the window, though the classroom was like a cave at night—even more depressing than during the day, its puckered cinderblock walls reflecting back on themselves in the dark glass. Even this late into winter, nearly March, she would still feel affronted by the early arrival of nighttime; it seemed as if she were being cheated, the way the day's gray sky went black by five-thirty or six. Jonna would stare at her reflection and think her face looked Munch-like and gaunt. She would smell her breath in her palm.

She would listen to the voices and footsteps in the hallway. She would brace herself. If the noises faded, marching onward past her room, she would let her shoulders relax. If the noises grew louder and someone peered in, speaking her name—*Mrs. Lorre?*—she would fight the urge to say, *Two doors down.* She would smile as she corrected the *Mrs.* to *Ms.*

She would like the parents full of nervous fidgeting or the ones who couldn't make eye contact more than the ones who brayed about their child's long-ago second-place finish in a fourth grade spelling bee, or the ones who referred to each other (*Honey, Doll, Bar-Bar*) or their kid (*Stevie, Benj, Our Gal*) with pet names.

She would try to explain the course, Business Level English, without saying, *It's for the dumb kids*. The process reminded her of a game she once played drunkenly in grad school where she had to describe Mickey Mouse without saying Mickey or Mouse or Disney or cartoon or ears. She would be interrogated. *Why did Frankie get a C- on his last paper? Why so many pop quizzes?* She would try to sound authoritative, using phrases like *striving toward performance benchmarks* and *creating an environment of learning and respect*. She would not reveal that this was her first job out of grad school, nor that she'd learned to bring a second blouse with her in the mornings, as she quickly pitted out the first one by the start of third period, nor that she had moved two thousand miles from home, lulled to the West Coast by Portland's cute public art and color-coded bus system, nor that she still barely knew her way around the gridded city, nor that she spent most of her time inert in her apartment, putting off trips even to the laundromat or the grocery store, wearing soiled stockings beneath her shoes and eating stale corn tortillas for breakfast, nor that she only had one friend here, a pug-nosed guy in the next apartment who wore tiresomely ironic t-shirts emblazoned with the names of landfills and nuclear power plants. She would clear her throat a lot.

Parents would grow angry, listing excuses for their children's poor performance and behavior: *Lannie has ADD; Jessie's father and I are going through a divorce; Belle always struggles in the winter*. They would make diffuse accusations: *Vince needs a certain sort of patience from his teachers; we just talked to Lucy's algebra teacher, and she's doing fine in there*. Jonna would try not to twitch. Her left eye was known to twitch under stress.

Everyone would shake hands at the end—all except the angriest, who might walk out without so much as a goodbye. Jonna would usher the rest back into the hallway—ladies in their creased slacks, men with their ties loosed from their collars—and feel slightly bruised and naked, even after the least contentious interactions. She would watch their steady retreat—a husband lightly placing his hand on the back of a wife's neck; a single woman rifling through her purse for her car keys—and feel a slick, fleshy panic. The doorknob—she would hang onto the doorknob as the parents rounded the corner of the hall, out of view—would grow warm and damp in her grip.

Wait, she would think each time, even with the surliest or most belligerent of the bunch, who now seemed so full of purpose as they headed back to their lives beyond these walls. *Where are you going?* she would want to know with the urgent injustice of a child left with the babysitter. *Take me with you.*

❧

All night, she'd been waiting for the Carkers. They were the seventh name on her list. She'd gotten through a weeping grandmother, two pissed-off dads, and three impatient couples. When they finally arrived, Mr. Carker turned out to be a bull-faced man, which didn't surprise Jonna. Mr. Carker's son was also bull-faced, with the same flat nose and wide nostrils, the same upper lip that seemed just short of a cleft palate—rising sharply at its midpoint and leaving the two front teeth partially exposed, even with a closed mouth. Just that—the insufficient coverage by the upper lip—left both father and son with a permanent expression of witless defiance.

Mr. Carker now paced slowly around the perimeter of Jonna's class-room, studying her Banned Books bulletin board, shaking his head in front of the index card about *The Adventures of Huckleberry Finn*. Jonna didn't know if this indicated his dislike of censorship or his dislike of her board. She clapped her hands softly to indicate it was time to begin; he ignored her.

Mrs. Carker was already sitting obediently at a student desk, playing with the program that had been handed out at the entrance of the school, rolling the corner of the bright green paper between her thumb and pointer finger. A full third of it was curled into a loose spiral. Jonna felt heartened by the inelegant curl; the same nervous tics that drove her mad with her students became suddenly reassuring when they came from the parents. *I could take her*, thought Jonna, as she assessed the woman's simple, cream-colored sweater and the noncommittal shimmer of her nail polish.

At the Current Events bulletin board, Mr. Carker fingered the famous picture of the president standing on the deck of an aircraft carrier in a flight suit. The paper wilted against its staples, the edges bowed forward from the thick heat of the school's old radiator system. "You talk politics in here?" he said. His voice was too loud for such a small room.

"No," Jonna said. "Well, yes. A lot of the reading we do is from magazines. Or newspapers."

"It's an English class. Not social studies." Mr. Carker said, still yelling. "When I was in high school, we read—" He paused for a moment. "Well, Dickens. I'm sure we read Dickens. And Kafka. The cockroach." He held his fingers into a claw, an apparent puppet of Gregor Samsa. Jonna tried to picture her class reading a book, these kids who sounded out words (and often incorrectly: *nostal-GUH, CHAY-os*), who carved up their desktops with nail files and cafeteria forks, who aspired to be NFL players or Navy Seals or, most commonly, nothing at all.

She gave him her speech on student anxiety about reading and how using nontraditional texts can lessen that anxiety. She was smiling as she talked. She sounded—even to her own ears—like a flight attendant or a salesgirl, someone whose job hinged on appeasement.

"Leonard likes current events?" Mr. Carker said as he fit himself into the student desk next to his wife, with the sort of unblinking eye contact that wavered between friendly and aggressive.

How strange to hear the boy called Leonard. Jonna had scarcely called him that since taking roll the first day, the rest of the class cackling and braying at the name. She hated the first day of the term, the way she was even less privy than usual to the in-jokes and elaborate sets of rules that seemed to knit together the chaotic, cruel fabric of high school. The first day was like being snowblind, pushing forward stubbornly and stupidly into the storm, unable to see even the outlines of a path. *Carker*, they all called him—a rough, barking name for the boy with the uneven haircut and strange mouth who sat in the back corner of the room, the last desk next to the window, staring straight ahead, erect in his chair like a soldier.

"Leonard," she told the Carkers now, "is inconsistent with current events. He is, overall, an inconsistent student. I'm having some problems with him." She'd been formulating this speech for weeks, and she searched for signs of recognition in their faces, any indication that they'd heard this before. But Mrs. Carker was unreadable. She had the sleepy sort of eyes that made her look dumbly affable or bored or both. Mr. Carker squinted at Jonna through thin slits.

"Listen," Jonna said, her voice rising suddenly and unevenly. The crackle of that one word—such an immature, adolescent noise—rendered her speechless and filled her with a rush of familiar feeling: that of losing her footing, of stumbling surely and clumsily away from the neatly ordered thoughts of moments ago.

❧

She had, by now, come to expect bad students. The incidents that had sent her home crying six months earlier—the boy who ripped up a midterm exam in front of her; the girl who threw her puck-like pencil eraser at Jonna's face when Jonna insisted the girl stand and read aloud; the chalk rendition that appeared on her board one day after lunch, with two watermelon-like orbs for breasts, a patch of white curlicues for pubic hair, and a sign atop saying, simply, *Bitch*—now made her only feel numb and slightly queasy. At worst, she would maybe pick through her dinner, unable to eat, but she fell asleep soundly even after the days when phlegmy spit dripped from her classroom doorknob or two boys passed what appeared to be a liquor bottle across the back row.

She'd come to understand these kids. They were bad because they were stupid. She'd learned about this in grad school: disruption due to discomfort in a standardized environment. The boy who ripped up his midterm had not even the most basic comprehension of a sentence, let alone a paragraph; whenever the girl with the eraser spoke, she tripped herself up in a painful riddle of tics and stutters. They knew on some fundamental level that they were inadequate, and the misbehavior was their clumsy, groping effort to attract attention away from that. Their ineffective attempt at misdirection. On most days Jonna felt as if she were standing in front of a room full of shitty magicians, none of whom had mastered sleight of hand.

Carker, though, was different. Carker unnerved her. He was quiet and unusually self-possessed. He had good posture. Rather than slouching with the listlessness of most of his classmates, Carker sat erect in his seat, as if a ruler measured his spine. In the beginning, Jonna had mistaken this for alertness, honing in on the boy the way she often did with the one or two students who might offset the apathy of an entire class. But the first time she asked him a question—*What do you think is this author's central argument?*—after they'd read a short editorial opposing a state sales tax, Carker simply stared at her. His hands were clasped on his desk, the photocopy of the editorial centered neatly in front of him. "Leonard?" she said, after a moment had passed without a response. "Carker?" she tried. He continued to look at her as if she were an animal in a zoo and not a particularly exotic one, maybe a goose or a ferret, something that asked for his attention but failed to interest him.

The class had shifted and giggled as Jonna stood in front of the room and Carker sat in the back, both silent now, staring at each other. Several students turned to look at Carker, but if he noticed, he gave no indication; his expression was as close to blank as one's could get while still awake, his features loose and impassive. Heat rose through Jonna's chest. She had grown familiar with the blustery hatching and scheming of her students, their fart noises and loudly dropped books. Quiet indifference unsettled her. "Carker?" she said one more time. Finally, he made a hissing noise, a low, wet sound between his teeth, as if he were declaring this standoff over, himself the winner. More giggles followed. Jonna eventually called on someone else, continued with her lesson, but for the rest of that day she couldn't get the image of the boy out of her head. Each time she flashed on him, the heat returned, as if she were revisiting a deep humiliation. Carker's empty face, and his sly, snaky noise held an unnamed challenge to it; she felt somehow found out, revealed.

For weeks after that she watched the boy, looking for even the slightest bobble in his veneer—a brow furrowed in thought, a nod of recognition, even a disgusted scowl. But his face never changed; it held the same seemingly alert yet empty expression day in, day out. She made it a point to stand in the doorway at the start of his particular class period, greeting each student (*Nice to see you again, Tracy. Don't you look awake today, Lawrence?*), some of whom said a tepid hello back, while others squinted skeptically or laughed in embarrassment. *Top of the morning to you*, she'd said once to Carker, inexplicably; it was the first corny phrase to pop into her head. He ignored her, walking past without pause.

Any time Jonna called on him, they had the same mute standoff. "Carker? Carker?" she would call, as if beckoning a lost dog. Each time, Carker sat and stared. The rest of the class laughed or made dramatic displays of trying not to laugh, as if Jonna had accidentally said *fuck* (which she hadn't let slip since her third week) or left a middle button undone on her blouse, exposing her pink demi-bra (which she guarded vigilantly against, after one unfortunate morning near the end of fall term).

Each night, as she rode the bus home, she would try to shake off her day and regain the wonder of her first few weeks here, when she was awed by the greenness of this city compared to Detroit's rusts and grays, its dramatic sweep of bridges over the Willamette, its elevated light rail gliding through downtown's Pioneer Square. Everything had seemed so precious and well appointed, and she'd felt large within it, like a giant in a dollhouse of a city. It was exhilarating, existing in a place that had not yet been inhabited by her or any of the messy trails of her history. No one in Oregon knew that Seth Greenblatt had stood her up for the senior prom, or that her mother had once drunkenly called her a *prissy bitch*, or that she'd unwittingly bled through her green capri pants on the third day of her trip across the country, discovering at a rest stop a stain that uncannily resembled the country of Spain and had left a deep pink imprint in her car's beige upholstery.

Now, though, when she cataloged the sites—the big pink building, the Made in Oregon sign, the purplish glow of the Hawthorne Bridge—they seemed already flat and disconnected from her, landmarks of some-one else's city. She was on her way from the muggy, airless room where she worked to the muggy, airless room where she lived. These were the moments, as rain drizzled down the bus windows and the person in the aisle next to her talked importantly into his cell phone and the two girls in the seat in front of her giggled together, when she thought of Carker. She pictured his ugly mouth or ridiculous bangs, or she wondered what he was doing right then. He bled like this into her thoughts, trailing her unbidden through this lonely, soulless city.

❧

"Leonard giving you problems?" Mr. Carker said, slouching awkwardly at his desk. Adults never fared well in these seats, Jonna knew. They sat hemmed in by the desktop soldered to the one of the metal arms. Mr. Carker kept repositioning himself to fit his knees beneath. Mrs. Carker swayed stiffly forward and back in hers, as if fearful of what she might catch were she to press too closely against any one surface. Jonna liked the gracelessness that the seats created, hoping it would keep the parents just uncomfortable enough to be docile.

"I can't tell what he's thinking," Jonna said. "He'll just sit there. Even when I call on him, he won't say anything."

Mrs. Carker said, "He can be *quiet* sometimes," with a voice as watery and thin as Jonna had imagined.

"It's more than that. I'm not really talking about quiet. He's pretty insolent," she said.

"Insolent?" Mr. Carker said slowly, as if he'd never heard the word before, let alone in conjunction with his son.

"Is he doing poorly?" Mrs. Carker stopped her swaying. Her husband rested his hand on her forearm, clasping it gently.

"It's not that simple," Jonna said. "He's a smart kid." In fact, she did not tell them, his writing revealed him to be uncommonly smart. While his sentences ran on from one to the next without even an attempt at punctuation, and his paragraphs were bloated and disorganized, his ideas were strong. In a stack of depthless papers about Afghanistan, while other students wrote thoughtlessly about terrorists and how bad it was for women to wear head scarves, Carker discussed the implications of US funding of the mujahideen in the 1980s; in a paper about sex ed, while many classmates railed against how uncomfortable condoms were and how uptight parents could be, Carker asked how those who opposed contraception answered to the question of global overpopulation.

"But?" Mr. Carker said.

"But he's quietly disruptive," Jonna said.

"How can you be quiet and disruptive?" Mr. Carker said.

"By having a general air of defiance," Jonna said, clasping her hands together in her lap. Her mouth felt dry. She wanted to cough or swallow, neither of which she did.

Mr. Carker said quickly: "We've never had any problems with Leonard. He's a good kid. Gets his work done. Minds us." He leaned forward in the desk now, as if to show he could crawl over the top of it to get to her, if need be.

"He's always gotten fine grades," Mrs. Carker added. "He passes every class." Her sleepy eyes were opened wider now, studying Jonna's face with an intent, unreadable expression. Was she issuing a challenge? A plea? She seemed to be sitting up straighter now, gaining sudden confidence.

"I'm not talking about passing," Jonna said. "It's likely Leonard will pass. I'm talking about a bad attitude which is infecting the classroom."

"Leonard's *infecting* people?" Mrs. Carker said.

"Look," Mr. Carker said, in a tone that suggested he was going to put an end to this silliness. "Leonard's a good kid. He's had a paper route since he was eleven. He watches his sister every day after school. Real good with her. Doesn't just sit her down in front of the television. Reads to her. Books."

"You should see the way he talks to her," Mrs. Carker said. "He never teases her or pokes her. He talks to her just like she's his same age."

They were clasping hands now, one of his and both of hers intertwined dramatically on his desk. "Used to be she had a hard time with the reading," Mr. Carker said. "But she's doing better now, since Leonard started with the books."

"That's nice," Jonna said dumbly. She was losing her momentum, as often happened in conferences, outmatched by the sheer, senseless force of parental love. With her grade book and detention slips, she was measly in comparison, a featherweight, half their age, with maybe a quarter of their conviction and loyalty.

She'd tried to avoid this altogether—the confrontation with the parents—by going directly to the boy instead. "Wait," she'd said to Carker one day, as his classmates filed out of the classroom. He backed himself against a wall, pressing into the concrete just next to the door, as if he hoped simply to slither out, unnoticed. From the hallway came rippling noises of students freed briefly and let loose upon each other, disparate shouts and the gleeful sort of laughter that often signaled a vicious bout of teasing. "I feel like there's some disconnect going on," she said. "Clearly you understand the material. But I'm not getting the sort of consistent participation I'd like to see. I don't think it's a learning issue. I think it's motivational."

Carker looked out the window. He seemed utterly at home in the gaping pauses of conversations. He stayed flat against that wall, even as the students from the next class began trickling in; he presented no resistance, no overt insolence, nothing Jonna felt she could point clearly to and punish.

"You're not presenting a problem," she stammered into his silence, "so much as a distinct lack. I think there's a lot more that you have to offer." Then, finally, more forcefully: "When I speak directly to you I expect a direct answer."

The students from the next class stared, open-mouthed, a few grinning, as if they'd lucked onto a particularly violent car wreck or public lynching.

"Okay," Carker said, but only, Jonna suspected, because he could sense that she was teetering on the edge of control. The word came out wispily, weightlessly, as if it were a cough or sigh, something that escaped his lips with little of his own volition.

And still nothing changed. The standoffs continued in class. The whole room quickened, grew altogether more alert and interested each time Jonna stood before them, trying to cajole Carker from his silence. She sensed, too, the other students beginning to be swayed by him. Classmates turned to gauge his response when Jonna announced a pop quiz or the due date of a writing assignment, as if he were the silent arbiter of classroom opinion. Sometimes, a wave of unaccountable snickering would ripple from his corner of the room. Jonna was never able to identify the source. As she surveyed the faces, most students fidgeted guiltily in their seats while Carker stared at her, empty.

If Jonna had had more self-control, she would've simply ignored him. But she found herself regularly checking his reaction as she lectured, her compass unaccountably drawn in his direction. It was like a tic she'd developed, glancing to the back right every few minutes. She was waiting for something, anything. But Carker remained utterly, improbably immobile. Little effort seemed required on his part, as if his stance were meditative, as if he'd successfully accomplished what they all longed for: wresting his mind from the physical shell that was forced into this desk fifty-five minutes a day. To each of Jonna's glances his way, his stillness seemed to be simply and unapologetically asking: *Who cares?* and *What does any of this matter?*

In graduate school, they'd talked about teaching as though they were training to be superheroes. *Reaching the unreachable* and *empowering the disenfranchised.* They talked about educational reform; they talked about multiculturalism; they talked about reframing the idea of learning disabilities into learning *differences.* Jonna received A's on everything. She student taught with an old, peach-faced woman who'd been teaching AP English forever and who regularly whipped her students into shouting frenzies over Ayn Rand's Objectivism or George Orwell's prescience about the current government. Jonna prepared meticulous lesson plans about Hobbesian philosophy and *Lord of the Flies* or naturalism in *Ethan Frome*, and the students lapped it up, taking furious notes in their loose-leaf binders with each word Jonna spoke.

She'd thought of all this during her first-term performance review. Shel Dougan, Brookswood's principal, had sat her down a few weeks before conferences and mixed several metaphors, talking about learning to walk before she could run and getting her feet wet and steadying her sea legs. He told her not to feel bad about the comments by veteran teachers after their classroom observations: *Ms. Lorre seems to have a tenuous grasp, at best, on classroom management strategies . . . Ms. Lorre appeared to have lost her train of thought more than once . . . Ms. Lorre seems to be easily intimidated by student resistance to the material.*

Jonna had stared past the principal's balding head into the student parking lot beyond his picture window. There were dual-cab trucks and all-wheel-drive wagons, row after row of shiny SUVs. She wondered which one was Carker's.

"It's not cause to worry," said Shel Dougan, in a tone that indicated otherwise.

"Look," Jonna said, pointing to four kids snaking through the lot, hunching low with their sweatshirt hoods tied around their heads. It was third period. Shel Dougan turned to look as they filed quickly into a beat-up Jeep. When he turned back to Jonna he looked tired, but he was also smiling, as if the two of them were in on some sort of a joke. She wasn't sure what that joke might be. The car peeled out from the lot. Shel Dougan held his hands up at his sides. "What can you do?" he said softly.

❦

Carker's parents were getting anxious and impatient; Jonna could see as much. The mother chewed on her bottom lip, the father tapped his foot loudly against the floor tiles.

"Tell me," Jonna said now, changing tactics. "What has Leonard told you about the class?"

Mrs. Carker shook her head. Mr. Carker shrugged. "Nothing," he said simply.

"We don't hear much," his wife added.

"Oh. Okay. All right," Jonna said, feeling a warm rush of disappointment. It was hard to imagine that he'd said nothing, not even a brief mention, a casual complaint or snide remark. She was flushed now, caught in the quiet embarrassment of the unrequited.

"I'm sure there's been some sort of misunderstanding," Mrs. Carker said, her voice steadily gaining strength. "Leonard would never be purposefully disrespectful."

"Damn right," Mr. Carker said—and then, quickly, "Pardon my French." He started in on a meandering story about a time in Boy Scouts when Carker helped some kids build a tent in the rain.

Jonna wasn't sure what to say. She'd hoped they'd be apologetic and complicit, worn down from years of disappointment and heartbreak. Their child, after all, was in Business Level English. Such a thing did not happen by accident, but after nearly continuous missteps and fuckups. She thought of her own parents; she did not often think of them, but conferences forced the issue, confronting her with hours of parents *not* her own. Jonna found it hard to imagine them like this: panicked and desperately defensive. The last contact she'd had was months ago when she'd called—frantic, unthinking— because she'd been unable to disarm a smoke alarm in her apartment, even after having doused the burnt pot of rice, yanked the alarm from the ceiling, and searched impotently for a battery compartment.

When her mother answered, her voice was slurred by gin. "Sweet-heart," she called Jonna, and "Doll." Her father shouted at her to rip out the battery and wouldn't concede when she insisted there was no compartment. He told her to stop being bull-headed and listen to him. She told him she was listening. The noise of the alarm was a piercing bleat. He told her rip the goddamn battery out. She said there was no battery compartment. He swore some more. She hung up and smashed the alarm with a hammer, gouging several deep divots in her already pocked hardwood floor.

Mr. Carker's story ended with his son saving a few other kids from catching pneumonia. He leaned forward at his desk now, looking smug and satisfied, as if he'd just made an unassailable point. "How long have you been at this?" he said. "We almost walked right past your room at first; we didn't realize you were the teacher." He was smiling, but Jonna heard the challenge in his voice.

Her cheeks grew warm. The wool of the suit was itchy on her arms through her thin blouse. "Long enough," she said. There was the slight-est quaver to her voice; she hated herself for it. Mr. Carker stared at her. She held his gaze for one beat, then another, finally looking past him to his son's desk—because that's what it had become, Carker's desk, even when it was empty.

She flashed on the class two Tuesdays ago when they'd been discussing an article claiming high school kids were being over-diagnosed with ADHD. Jonna thought the topic would be popular, given how many of her students faithfully visited the school nurse to receive their Ritalin or Adderall or

Dexedrine. But they sat square-jawed and yawning, doodling in their note-books, resting their heads heavily in their hands.

"If this author visited Brookswood, would the visit confirm or challenge his opinion?" Jonna asked. She was in front of her desk, leaning against its edge, somewhere between sitting and standing, her hands clasped loosely at her waist. It was the pose she remembered from her own English teachers, one of friendly, casual confidence, as if they'd all just gathered here to chat. Bryn Martin cracked her gum loudly in the front row. Justin Scott kicked at the floor, his gym shoes making short, sharp squeaks against the tiles. Carker sat in the back, blankly watching her.

"Anyone?" Jonna said. "Lorraine?"

Lorraine Ingram—greasy hair, third row—looked up from her desk, blinking quickly, as if Jonna had just slapped her. "I don't know. Confirm?"

"Why do you say confirm?"

Lorraine shrugged. She sat for a long time, as if she were thinking. "I don't know. Challenge?"

"Why challenge?" Jonna said, trying to keep her voice even and well modulated.

"What was the question again?" the girl said.

"Dumbass," Roger LeBron whispered from the next row.

"And what's your opinion on this, Roger?" Jonna said quickly.

"Lots of people I know doped up on speed," he said. He had the craggy, asymmetrical face of someone who'd been beaten up a lot.

"And what do you make of that?" Teaching, Jonna had discovered, was mostly weaving together flimsy filaments of thought and then acting as though the result created something of substance.

"Don't make anything of it," Roger said.

"Does anyone make anything of that?" she called out, watching the roomful of eyes watching her. The wall heater made its rhythmic ticking noise; the air felt thick and unwashed. She could taste the yellow flecks of chalk in the back of her throat, feel them on her fingertips and in her hair. That soft yellow powder was pervasive, inescapable. Jonna found it on the seat of her car, the faucet in her bathroom at home, her pillowcases and sheets—the shadow of this room following her everywhere.

"Anyone?" she repeated. "How about Sam?" she finally said. "Sam, what do you think?"

She had come to rely on Sam Larimer—and a few other students like him—in this way, as a rescue. He was a stick-thin, zit-faced, hardworking kid who ran his finger beneath the lines of words as he read aloud, cleared his throat incessantly, and pressed so hard when he wrote that he often broke off the tips of his pencils and had to use the sharpener over and over again. These quirks—along with a history of related quirks, Jonna suspected—left Sam open to merciless teasing. Each time he went to the sharpener, he was pelted with spitballs. *Pencil dick*, they called him. The mocking only seemed to become worse if Jonna yelled at them to stop, like trying to discourage a swarm of bees by swatting at them. So she watched impotently as Sam got torn to bits, and she tried to make up for it by writing encouraging notes on his essays and frequently soliciting his opinions, which he always framed proudly in stiff, bookish terms: "Well, it appears patently obvious to me that . . . " or "I am of the mind that . . ." He only lost his train of thought occasionally, as classmates coughed loud insults into their fists.

"Sam, do you think kids are being over-diagnosed with behavioral disorders?" she asked him now. He was good for deflecting attention away from Jonna, if only because he was the one person in the room less liked than she was.

Sam began to open his mouth, then suddenly stopped. His eyes darted in one direction, then another; his hands fluttered quickly in his lap. He took a deep breath and came to a strange sort of halt, sitting almost still, staring at Jonna. His face was nervous, though, the corner of his lip pulsing like a heartbeat.

"Sam?" Jonna said.

The boy continued to stare at her. He sealed his lips tightly together, as if in a dramatic display of *buttoning it*. For a moment, Jonna was confused; she continued to repeat his name, and he continued to sit. Someone began chuckling, and another few students let out low whooping noises. Roger LeBron called out, "Sammy!" in a tone far less mocking than usual. Jonna was only one beat slower than the rest of them in realizing what was happening. Sam sat up straighter in his chair now, shifting his narrow shoulders back, staring straight ahead, as the hum of noise grew around him. He was, she saw now, trying to pull a Carker. His lips were still pressed tightly together, but now they suppressed a grin. Jonna felt a hot, thick anger, and a desire to slap the kid across his zitty red cheek. He'd sold her out.

She looked involuntarily to the back corner by the window, and there Carker sat, his mouth also spread thinly across his face in the tiniest little smile. The expression was odd, almost creepy. She'd never seen Carker smile before.

"Leonard . . ." Her voice was shaky, but loud, ". . . what is your opinion on this?" She couldn't even remember her original question. She marched toward the back of the classroom, toward his desk. "What do you have to say about it all?" She was yelling. Carker stared at her, with the same bemused expression. She stood right next to his desk, watching the slow, even rise and fall of his striped t-shirt.

"Leonard! Why don't you grace the class with your opinion? Care to open your mouth, or would you prefer to sit back here on high?" She was spitting. The wet spray flew through the air, some landing on Carker's desk, some glistening on his cheek. He didn't wipe it away. The room was silent. Jonna didn't know if she'd ever heard it so quiet. "You think you could do better?" she yelled, waving toward the front of the classroom. She knew she was acting crazily, but she felt a light, buzzy sensation in her chest, as if she were coming up for breath after a long time submerged. "You think you can do better than me, Leonard?" she yelled. "Go for it!" She was standing so close, she could smell his fishy mouth from the cafeteria lunch. He had something pale and fleshy caught between his front two teeth. "Go for it!" she yelled, and for a moment there was nothing, just quiet all around her.

Jonna made a sudden starting motion, as if she might head-butt Carker, and he flinched. She was deeply satisfied by that. She hung there, inches from his face, as his smile faded. Carker had a scrawny little chest, Jonna realized. He also had a light patch of freckles beneath his left eye. She fought to hold her pose; there was, she deduced, no going back from this. Her breath was coming through her nostrils in a forceful rush. A slight tingling had begun to travel up the back of her neck, from the strange angle of it. She was about to buck forward again, to see if he would flinch again—

it was the only thing she could think of—when the boy finally, thankfully, raised both arms in the air as if in surrender.

He stood up slowly from his desk and slipped past her, his face bright and full of color. Carker walked to the front of the room—it was more of a shuffle, his feet sliding heavily against the floor, his hands tucked in his pockets, his head bent forward. He looked suddenly different than usual—looked younger, his shoulder blades poking through the back of his shirt like a pair of parentheses. Jonna felt a quick flash of uncertainty. She eased into the empty desk next to Carker's; Liz Lopshire's, an unfortunate girl often absent due to a bleak cocktail of asthma and allergies. When Carker got to the front of the room, he slouched against her desk. He was all curves now—the slope of his back, the bend of his neck, his loose, liquid arms—a pale imitation of his normal ramrod self.

"Go ahead!" Jonna yelled. The boy moved his lips, as if he was going to say something, but no sound came out.

The rest of the class was caught between excitement and confusion, some kids leaning forward in their seats to gawk at Carker, others twisting around to look at Jonna, most shifting between the two, forward and back, trying to take in the whole situation. A rippling anticipation moved through the seats. Wordless noises came from the crowd—a cawing laugh, a low, grunting, question-like sound. But no one said anything. Everyone was waiting.

Finally, Carker ran his fingers once through his uneven haircut and said, "How many of you are on drugs?" His voice was low, but surprisingly uneven, the last word coming out in a breathy squeak.

The class laughed.

"Prescription drugs?" Carker said quickly, his face reddening more deeply.

Hands went up.

"Donovan," Carker said, pointing to one. "What're you on?"

The boy listed several drugs, his voice crackling. Donovan Barrett had barely spoken all term. Carker's voice grew a little louder as he asked, "How many of you have to talk to a shrink?" Hands went up in the air. Leslie Torneau talked about a therapist who recommended hospitalization when she was eleven. Carker nodded. "How old were you when you first saw a shrink?" he asked, and "Who wanted you to go, you or your parents? Do the drugs even make you feel better?" Mike Johannsen said he crushed up his slow-release capsules for a better buzz. Barrett Glenn once stole a few of his mom's Valium, which helped him relax and get his work done.

These weren't kids who normally talked. The air of conspiracy that usually thrummed just below the surface, between Carker and the rest of them, had been let loose. They were—all of them—giddy with sudden power.

Soon, Carker began imitating Jonna. "What conclusion can we draw from that?" he said in a high-pitched voice—one of her standard lines. He never once looked her way. Other students, though, kept peering back, looking for her reaction, maybe waiting for her to put a stop to this and regain control. But she just sat, awash in this stifling room with its muddied floor tiles and fingerprint-stained windows and littered mess of papers and candy wrappers and pen caps underfoot.

"What you're telling me," Carker said from the front of the class, swooshing his arms through the air like a conductor, "is you're a bunch of addicts." Everyone laughed. Jonna could taste shame in her throat, hot and metallic. But beneath it lay something else, something pulsing and distinct: it was relief, the bright and certain relief of sitting back in the cheap seats, at just the slightest remove—six measly rows, but it felt right now like a chasm—from the pressure, the performance, the small, small life she'd so quickly amassed up there in front of these little animals.

Carker went on.

Mr. Carker was calling her *ma'am* now. Jonna was only half listening, gleaning a few parts of sentences here and there. "I understand a room full of them must be a handful, ma'am . . . We've been pretty lucky with him, ma'am . . ." His wife sat with the thinnest, stiffest smile, as if she'd been posing for a picture for several beats too long.

Jonna was sick to death of parents. Their love seemed valueless, devoid of any balance or scale, if even the rotten kids were swaddled protectively by it. She imagined the way Mrs. Carker tucked her son's hair behind his ear at the breakfast table, and Mr. Carker playfully punched him in the shoulder as they sparred about which baseball team would win the pennant this year. She wondered about the pet names they might have of him and what predictable pictures they had framed along the staircase—Carker as a naked baby, Carker in his Sunday best, Carker in his Little League uniform, Carker posed with his sister and parents in wicker chairs against a fake blue background in some downscale department store photo studio.

Jonna had, since two Tuesdays ago, successfully ignored Carker. Or at least successfully appeared to be ignoring him. She never called on him, never looked at him. But she felt him from his corner, like a lamp turned up too brightly, its bulb heating her face. And the rest of the class hadn't yet righted itself. Sam Larimer still refused to talk. Donovan Barrett was sent to the office after calling her an asshole. A half-dozen kids, in a strikingly premeditated act of disobedience, wrote *Don't know don't care* across the latest reading quiz.

There was a rapping at her door. Jonna saw the faces of the next parents through the chicken-wire window. She looked at her list and saw that they belonged to Debbie Trainor, who had prominent buck teeth and regularly forgot to write verbs into her sentences. Jonna had nine more sets of parents to meet after them. There was a deep throbbing at the base of her neck, as if it might simply snap from her shoulders, sending her head rolling across the mucky floor. She was not altogether put off by the image.

She held one finger up to the Trainors. *Wait, please.*

"Well," Mr. Carker said, disentangling himself from his desk. "We won't keep you." Mrs. Carker followed his lead, and Jonna had no other choice but to stand.

How long she'd been waiting to meet them. How sure she'd been that they—by their very existence—would provide answers about the boy. But now they stood inches away from her, Mr. Carker with a mole in front of his right ear, his face pale like winter, and Mrs. Carker with her unassuming middle-aged haircut, short gray-flecked layers around the face with a blow-dried lift at the top. Neither of them offered her anything. And now they were trying to leave. Jonna felt twisted around and jarred loose, like at the abrupt moment of waking from a dream of freefall.

"Wait," she said. Her voice sounded like a child's. "Please. Sit."

Mrs. Carker looked to her husband to take the lead. Jonna did the same. What was it, she wondered, with the fucking men in this family? Slowly, though, he sat, faintly shaking his head. His wife sat, too. Jonna remained standing.

For one long beat, then another, she just stared at them, trying to collect herself. *This isn't easy for me*, she imagined beginning. But there was, she'd tell them, something seriously wrong with their son. *Ser-i-ous-ly*, she would repeat, elongating each syllable. He was antisocial to the point of being maladaptive. Or maybe she would say he shows no concern for the well-being of others. Or maybe both. He was malicious, mean-natured and dangerous, she would tell them, punctuating each word with a gesture—a finger pointed directly at them or her hands clapping softly together. He had, she would continue, sociopathic tendencies. His intelligence, rather than being an asset, was hazardous to others. To the *safety* of others, she might emphasize, depending on their reactions. He was powerful and shouldn't be underestimated, she'd say, pausing to let the words sink in, but only for a brief moment—not long enough to let them begin a defense.

Their boy was sick, she would continue. She liked that word, sick. Maybe she'd repeat it. He needed some sort of intervention, she'd say—counseling or medication or a strong cocktail of the two. They should not delay. They should get help as soon as possible.

Here she would pause a final time, possibly walking behind her desk to lean her hands on it as she searched for the perfect metaphor. Leonard was, she'd say, a ticking bomb, an undetonated landmine, a sniper lying in wait.

The Carkers, she knew, would dismiss her claims, Mr. Carker likely yelling, Mrs. Carker crying. They'd storm out, maybe write her a nasty letter, complain to Shel Dougan and then to Dustin Lourdes, head of the school board. They'd go home and hold Carker tightly, pet his head, speak cooing, reassuring words into his ear. Maybe they'd finally buy him that PlayStation 2, or schedule that long-promised trip to Disneyland. They would joke quietly with each other—safely out of the children's earshot—about what a nut that teacher had been. They'd spin their fingers next to their ears. Cuckoo. Cuckoo.

But the next time Carker pulled his sister's hair, the next time he broke curfew, the next time he sulked through dinner, they would wonder. There would be a tiny sliver of doubt. Jonna would have planted the seed, would have begun to wrest him from them, them from him.

The Trainors knocked again on the door. Jonna held up her entire hand this time: *Stop*. They could wait their turn. The words—bitter, violent, sudden as vomit—were coming.

Joyless Men

NICK HEALY

THE TELEPHONE WOKE ME JUST AFTER MIDNIGHT. I HELD TIGHT TO THE covers for one ring, then another. I figured the call could only be one of two things—bad news or a wrong number—and wanted to ignore it. But I rolled across the side of the bed once occupied by my wife and plucked the receiver from the nightstand, where she used to keep a pile of books about how to better enjoy life. I cleared my throat and said hello.

"Forgive me for calling, Carl." The voice on the other end came through slowly and quietly. "This is Peter Johnson."

"Pete?"

"Johnson," he said, "Mary's husband."

"Pete, I know who you are." The Johnsons had been our neighbors for almost twenty years, and they'd lived on Arona Street for ten years before we came along. Everyone on the block knew them by name and by sight—the fat lady and the stick man—and knew that Mary had gone off to a nursing home last year.

"Fine," he said. "I could use your help about now."

"I'm half asleep, Pete. It's the middle of the night. What's the trouble?"

It was true that neither Pete nor Mary had ever been anything but kind to me, my wife Nan, and our two girls. They were good neighbors. They kept a spare key for us, picked up our papers when we'd gone up north, and reminded us to get our leaves out to the curb a day before the city crew was scheduled to come and take them away.

It was also true that I had said cruel things about Pete and his wife, that I had looked at them through our windows and uttered whatever coarse jokes came to mind. When Mary took their gray terrier Linus for a walk, I compared the leash to a tether on the great Hindenburg, destined to explode before stunned onlookers. I suggested Pete and Linus were on borrowed time, that eventually Mary would get hungry enough to eat them, too. And I took to calling Pete's wife Maryland, the woman whose ass was large enough to merit statehood.

Our girls, always immobile in front of the television in our living room, didn't often laugh at my gags, but they latched onto the nickname. Everyone in our house—even my wife, who accused me of being crude and unkind—used it in our private conversations. The girls spread it to other neighborhood kids, and I assume those kids brought it home to their parents. My wife worried that Pete or Mary would find out. She tried to get us all to stop saying it, but the day they took Pete's wife away, Nan called me at the office and said, "Maryland had a stroke. It took four paramedics to carry her out of the house."

§

I pulled a pair of blue jeans and a heavy sweater over my flannel pajamas, and I wiggled some wool socks over the tube socks I'd worn to bed. In the foyer, I stepped into my boots, zipped my parka snug to my chin, tugged a stocking cap down to my eyebrows, yanked on my leather gloves, picked up my keys, and hurried outside. I'd promised Pete I could get to the city lockup in fifteen minutes, no more than twenty.

Snow, packed hard on the front walk, groaned and cracked beneath the rubber soles of my boots. Each step produced a clean and loud sound like the snapping of a thick twig, which echoed down the block and bounced off the dark houses.

I worried that the racket of my minivan—the roar from its rusted muffler and the whine of its cold belts—might wake the neighbors, and some of my wife's cronies might peek out to see me driving off and then whisper to her about my strange comings and goings in the middle of the night, hound-dogging around town with God only knows who.

The streets were empty in our neighborhood and mostly the same when I crossed into Saint Paul, cut through Como Park, and headed downtown.

This sort of cold kept people, including the riffraff, off the streets. I figured that had made Pete an easy mark for the cops, who were probably bored half stiff even in the middle of Frogtown, long the part of the city where people went looking for unlawful thrills. That was where Pete had gotten into his trouble. On the phone he hadn't been forthcoming with the details. He said only that the police had stopped him with some "young lady" in his car.

Once the van warmed up, I didn't mind being out. The world looks different when the temperature drops so far below zero. Everything takes on a crispness and tidiness. Salt and slush harden into a dry white film on the asphalt. The glow of each streetlight forms a distinct umbrella. The trails of smoke from chimneys and tailpipes swirl in tight curls and then disappear. To be out in that weather—when all other creatures had hidden themselves away—made me feel bold and strong, even though I rode inside the warm shell of a rumbling machine.

I tried to imagine Pete cruising for a Frogtown pro—that's what most lonely guys went down there for—but it didn't add up. I envisioned him rolling down his window to talk to the girl and a rush of cold air swooshing in, stirring his nerves and causing him to fumble with words. The Pete I knew wouldn't have had the first idea what to say, how to go about it.

Lots of people have secret lives, little parts of themselves they keep hidden away, but Pete wasn't the sort of guy to be cruising Frogtown. I knew that in the way I knew he loved Maryland, that he had never once been embarrassed by her. I knew because for all those years I had watched them together, noticed the way he looked at her, and heard how he spoke to her. Pete was good even in his secret places.

When she left a week before Halloween, Nan said she and the girls were going to stay with her mother and that she didn't know when they would be back. When I asked why, she droned a list of the ways I had let her down and made her feel unloved.

"You have become a joyless man, Carl." The girls were waiting in Nan's car when she said this. "Don't you want to change that? Don't you want something better? For yourself, I mean? Or for all of us?"

"We've been together for twenty years," I said. "We had six months of infatuation, but since then, we've been pretty much the same as we are now. That's how couples are. That's how marriage is."

"That's a marriage, huh? You tell me you've been bored for nineteen and a half years, and you expect this to make me feel better?" Nan had her hair in a ponytail, like she'd worn all the time back in college, but it was darker now and streaked with gray. "What do you know about marriage?"

We stood in the foyer and stared at each other. Nan had her hand on the doorknob. I thought about reaching out and taking her arm—gently, in a way that would only say that I didn't want her to go. But all I could see in her face and her tired shoulders was the wear of the years, and I couldn't think of a good reason for her to stay.

"I only know what our marriage has taught me," I said. "I thought you knew the same. I thought we were on the same page."

Nan's top lip curled and shivered, and she spoke in bursts. "You know shit. You know shit about marriage. You know shit about me."

She cranked the knob, jerked open the door, and backed over the threshold.

"The same page? That's great, Carl." Her hip held open the storm door. Nan leaned back inside and spoke softly again. "I was never on that page."

The streets of downtown Saint Paul always went quiet after business hours, and they were especially so after midnight. The cold and emptiness made the place look unreal—like a painted backdrop at the old Palace Theater, where the marquee was dark when I drove past. The Christmas lights that city workers strung along the boulevards each year had been shut off, too, and no cars were parked outside the jailhouse.

I left my van running and hurried across the sidewalk. A bank sign said the temperature had sunk down near twenty below. The air tightened the skin on my face, hardened the short curls of my beard, dried my sinuses, and jolted my lungs with an energy that felt almost like youth. I slowed near the doorway to look at the stout old towers in that corner of the city. Everything looked clean and sturdy—beautiful, I thought. Still, I couldn't wait to get inside.

The lobby of the jail was dim and cramped, not at all like I had expected, and it reeked of microwave popcorn. A young cop—a woman—sat alone behind a counter. No one else was around. The officer's name badge said *Vang*. She held up one finger, smiled with tight lips, chewed a few times, and swallowed.

"Sir," she said. "You can't leave your van running out there."

I glanced back at the doorway, wondering how the hell she'd know that, and gave her a curious look. She tapped her finger on top of the closed-circuit monitor on her desk.

"I'll only be a minute," I said. "I've come for Peter Johnson, my neighbor. How do I get him sprung from this place?"

"You can't leave an unattended vehicle on the street with the motor running."

Officer Vang was a pretty and tiny thing. She couldn't have been more than five feet tall, and I guessed she'd been on the force a short time. She could have been no older than twenty-three or twenty-four. She had smooth skin on her cheeks and eyes of the darkest brown, knowing eyes for someone so young.

"Oh, it'll be okay," I said. "What sort of a nut would try to steal a vehicle from outside the county jail?"

"The kind who'd rather nab a nice warm piece of junk than spend the night freezing to death outside." She smiled again, wider this time, and I could see a small flake of popcorn hull wedged in her lower teeth.

"Look," I said. "Pete—my neighbor—has had a rough night already, and he's an older guy. It would be nice for him to get into a warm car, don't you think? Maybe you'd keep lookout for me?"

She rolled her eyes, pressed a button on her desk, and nodded toward the door over her shoulder. I walked to the door and thanked her before I headed into the back.

"I take no responsibility for that van," Officer Vang said.

It was true there were good reasons for Nan to leave me, but she didn't know what they were. There had been another woman—one other woman. That was eight or nine years earlier, and Nan had never found out.

Mee was no older than Officer Vang when she came to work in my department—back when I was doing marketing for one of those Internet companies that was going to make everyone rich. Her face was lean, cheekbones high and long. She wore gray most days, and the color suited her black hair and dark eyes. She chose tight blouses and short skirts, like all the women on television wore at the time. She looked to me like the opposite of Nan. Where Nan was pink or pale or soft, Mee was brown or dark or firm. I watched her every day, stared at the profile of her body while she microwaved her Lean Cuisines in the break room, and eyed her backside as she hurried back and forth from meeting after meeting. She didn't seem to mind.

Still, it wasn't easy to have an affair. It didn't *just happen*, like people always say. It took work and persistence. I embarrassed myself, changed my mind a hundred times, went to sleep next to Nan full of guilt before I ever laid a hand on Mee.

But when the chance finally came, I felt only thrill while I glided my hands over her unfamiliar body and at last saw the color of her nipples, the faint treasure line below her bellybutton, and the arc of her bare hip. I pulled her against me, groped her, and squeezed her until she finally said, "Easy, Carl. Be easy with me."

When I climbed on top of her, I moved delicately until Mee hooked her legs around me and pulled my body hard against hers. Then there was no more going easy. I was happy, and during those few times we had together, I felt the thing I had once mistaken for love.

Officer Vang's chair was empty when Pete and I came into the lobby, after I had bailed him out, helped him collect his belongings, and gotten the details on how he could recover his impounded car in the morning. I stopped and looked at the monitor on Officer Vang's desk, where I could see her shooing a large man in a long coat away from my van. I led Pete across the lobby, and we met Officer Vang in the doorway—her hands balled in front of her chest, jaw clenched, and eyes wet from the cold. She reached out with one fist and slapped my ring of keys into my palm.

She said, "What did I tell you?" and headed inside. I tried to apologize, but she only nodded and kept going.

I followed her back toward her desk, while Pete stood at the door and waited like a small child—rocking from the balls of his feet to his heels, toasty warm inside his puffy down coat, which he wore with a woolen scarf, cap, and gloves.

I leaned on the counter and spoke softly to Officer Vang.

"That's Pete Johnson." I tilted my head in his direction. "We live out in Falcon Heights, just north of the city. You know where that is?"

"I do," she replied.

"I've known Pete for years, and this is the first time he's had any sort of trouble."

Officer Vang craned to see around me and looked Pete up and down.

"Do you know what Pete was in for?" I asked.

"I don't," she said. "They must have told you when—"

"Sure they did. Of course. They picked him up in Frogtown. He had a young woman in his car, a certain type of woman, if you know what I mean."

"I do," she said, and I could tell she was trying not to smile.

I nodded at Officer Vang and gave her a look that said we understood each other. She was putting up a tough front, but I thought she seemed sweet and smart and sly in some way—a little like Mee had been. I hoped she might think well of me, but I realized that when she looked at me she didn't see the person I used to be. She saw thinning hair on top of my head and a messy beard on my chin; she saw the extra inches around my middle. She saw a middle-aged man alone in the world.

Behind me, Pete cleared his throat and said, "Ah, Carl. Could we get on our way now?"

His eyes were bloodshot, and the lines beneath them formed dark rings that stretched down near his cheekbones.

"I'm sorry," I said. "I was just checking to see if Officer Vang here has any suggestions regarding who a guy may want to talk to about clearing up this little misunderstanding."

Pete sighed and said, "I'd like to get on home."

I arched my eyebrows and spoke quietly to the officer. "What do you say? Do you have any friends who might get a harmless old man off the hook?"

"I don't. It doesn't work that way," she said. "But if he's a first-timer, he'll just pay a fine for soliciting. No big deal."

A few summers back, Pete and Maryland had celebrated their fortieth wedding anniversary. They'd never had any children, so they threw themselves a backyard party and invited all the neighbors, even the young couples who'd moved to the block only recently and hadn't made much effort to get to know anyone.

Nan volunteered to bring dessert, and she conspired with several other neighbors to surprise Maryland by baking a three-tiered wedding cake—with lemon between the layers of each tier, just like Pete said they'd had at their wedding. Everyone clapped when the women carried the cake outside. They set it down on a picnic table, and next to the cake, Nan propped a framed photo from Pete and Maryland's wedding.

When the party was winding down, Nan sliced all but the top tier of the cake and sent pieces home with anyone who would take one. She told Maryland to take the top tier inside, to share it with Pete some other time, and we cleared off the picnic table.

I picked up the photograph and gave it a good long look. In it, Maryland was just a skinny thing. Her face was angular—her cheeks hollow and her chin solid. She wore a wide, open-mouthed smile. Tiny creases marked the corners of her eyes, which were round and bright. *Look at her*, I thought. *Look how beautiful she was.*

Nan said, "Gorgeous, wasn't she?"

I should have agreed—because it was as true as anything—but I made a joke instead.

"Just think," I said. "Now that girl and five of her little friends could camp out in one of Maryland's dresses."

Nan gave a heavy sigh, and I thought I saw tears in her eyes when she turned away.

"What?" I said. "Come on, Nan."

She walked toward the house and didn't look back.

In the van, Pete kept mostly quiet. He thanked me for coming, which he'd already done twice in the jailhouse, and he said he was grateful to have a neighbor he could trust to be discreet, a clever way of asking me to keep my mouth shut.

I wasn't going to tell anybody, but I figured I had a right to know the whole story, which neither Pete nor the cops had taken the time to share. So I asked him to spill the beans.

"You know the facts of it," he said.

"Not really. I know what the cops say you did, but I don't know what you thought you were doing, what on Earth moved you to go down to Frogtown and pluck yourself a hooker off a street corner."

He only sighed and faced the passenger-side window.

I had taken a different route home, cutting over north of Como Lake and passing through the neighborhood where Nan grew up. She had taken me there when we first started going together, because she wanted to introduce me to her parents and show me the streets of her childhood. After we got married, we decided to buy a house nearby so she could be close to home, but her parents sold their place and moved to a new townhouse on a golf course a few years later.

Pete looked at the passing houses as if he'd never traveled those streets before, and he stayed quiet. Soon we crossed the empty avenue that formed the border between Saint Paul and Falcon Heights. I turned onto Arona and stopped in front of Pete and Maryland's house. He unclipped his seatbelt and thanked me again for helping out.

"Look, Pete, your business is your business. But don't you think you ought to fill me in so I can at least know what secrets I'm keeping?"

He had his fingers on the door latch. He could have gotten right out and walked away if he wanted to, but he sat back and looked me straight in the eye for the first time that night. He pushed his stocking cap off his forehead and smoothed his eyebrows, which had grown long and wild. Since Maryland went to the nursing home, he'd had a general messiness about him—nose and ear hair unchecked, fingernails long and dirty.

"Maybe we can figure a way out of this," I said.

"Honestly," he said. "You know the long and short of it. There isn't much more to tell."

"Just give me the story."

Nan and I screwed for the first time on the floor of her apartment over near the University. We'd been together for a month. It was the dead of summer—a long and hot one—and all we wanted to do was lie around in front of the fan. We played tapes on her roommate's boom box, drank a few cans of Stroh's, and talked all day. I told her everything about myself. I told her which cartoons I'd watched as a kid, how old I was when I tried my first cigarette, why I hated the Beatles, and why at fifteen I'd lied to my friends about losing my virginity. She told me about the old records her father used to play, why she'd been fired from her first part-time job (selling candy at a movie theater), and how when she was thirteen she had let an older boy put his hand down her pants on the school bus one day.

We stripped off our clothes piece by piece as the afternoon wore into evening and the brick building began to give off a heat of its own. Down to our underwear, we lay on our sides, looked at each other's skin, and rested a hand on each other's hip. We were talked out, and I believed that we had arrived at something, that we had created a connection by sharing our stories, by telling the truth. As if that's all people meant when they talked about falling in love.

When we got out of our underwear and Nan slid herself down onto me, I decided the talk might have meant nothing. I figured love was just a polite name for the kick we got when we put our bodies together, which we did again and again until our sweat soaked the carpet and our backs glowed with red patches of rug-burn.

＊

The truth was, Pete said, Maryland had never gone down on him, and he didn't want to go to his grave without knowing what it felt like.

It was not the sort of thing he'd thought much about over the years, but with his wife in a nursing home and nobody in the house with him, Pete's lonely mind wandered. For some reason—and he didn't know why—he decided that cold and miserable night that he was going to do something about it. He drove to Frogtown, where everybody who has ever drawn a breath in Saint Paul knows you can't swing a dead cat without hitting a hooker or a dealer, and he drove up and down each block until he saw a woman alone on a corner. She smiled at him when he slowed near the curb.

"She gets in and says *What do you want, mister? Do you want this? Do you want that? How much you got?* She talks so fast I can hardly keep up," Pete said. "So I gave her an answer, and she told me to pull into this alley and stop the car."

The woman kissed Pete on the cheek and asked for the money up front. He paid—twenty bucks was all—and she unzipped his pants. The moment she slipped her hand into his shorts, a bright light shined on them.

"Then I see men running at the car," Pete said. "I don't know if they are going to kill us both or what in heck they have in mind. Then, lickety-split, they yank us both out of the car, pat us down, lock on the handcuffs, and take us to squad cars."

"They were watching you all along," I said. "You were a sitting duck."

"Sure, and you don't know the half of it."

There was another woman up front in the squad car, sitting on the passenger side. She introduced herself and said she was a reporter from the *Pioneer Press*. She said she wanted to know why men like Pete did what they did.

"No way in hell," I said. "Please tell me you gave her the dementia routine."

"What's that?"

"You know, 'Where am I? Who are you? Wasn't that my niece?'"

Pete gave me a bashful grin and shook his head. He leaned forward, grabbed the latch on the door again, and pulled it open.

"No. I told her what I'd done and why. No point hiding it anymore."

The truth was, we had a good marriage. We were together five years before our first daughter was born, and we would not have had children at all if we weren't optimistic about the future. We had our second girl two years later, even though the first had tested us in all kinds of ways we never expected. We got along. We pulled each other through. That's all a person can expect in a marriage.

But Nan could never be realistic. She was always putting her nose in another book written by some psychologist she'd heard on the radio or seen on TV. She was always finding new ways to describe our shortcomings as a couple or as a family and new prescriptions for us to lead lives that were more filled with *joy*. That was a big word in those books. *Joy*.

Once I said, "Look around you, Nan. Do you see a world filled with joyful people? Do you see people prancing along and grinning from ear to ear?"

We were in bed, and she had been explaining how we needed to better appreciate the wonders of daily life, to find the joy in common things.

"It's not about how you behave, Carl. It's about how you feel inside." Nan set her book aside, propped herself on one elbow, and clicked off the lamp. "It's about making a genuine life that brings you true happiness."

We lay silently in the dark. I knew she had satisfied herself, that she was pleased she had set me straight again.

"You know something, Nan," I said. "I am happy—not every day, not all the time, but most of the time. I am generally a happy person, and I wish you were, too."

That was the truth. I was happy—with her, with our family, and with our home. I hadn't always done or said the right things, and there were lots of times when I wished hard for something new, something different. But it occurred to me finally that a life with another person could only be so good, that we should expect one other human being to give us only so much of what we want. If we can give each other good company and a bit of security, why do we have to ask for more?

That night in the dark, Nan whispered, "I am happy, Carl. I am."

I knew it was a lie, but I didn't say so.

I brought Pete to the impound lot first thing in the morning, left him at the pay booth, and headed straight for the *Pioneer Press* building. When I asked to see the reporter who had been riding around with the cops last night, the young woman at the front desk looked at me like I'd gone out of my head.

"I'm here for my neighbor," I said. "He's a mixed-up old man. He's not the sort who goes around picking up teenage hookers. He doesn't deserve to have his name all over the newspaper."

The receptionist said she didn't have a clue what I was talking about and she couldn't help me if I didn't have a name. I asked to use her phone and if she wouldn't mind looking up the number of the county jail. She dialed the number and handed me the receiver. A deep-voiced man answered, and when I asked for Officer Vang, the girl who worked the front desk, he said she was off duty until the evening, which I should have figured. Neither he nor anybody handy at the jail knew about any reporter being around the night before. I hung up and pleaded with the receptionist to help me out.

"Look," I said, "somebody around here has to be in charge of this reporter, whoever she was. One of the editors must know something about the story."

The woman at the desk frowned, picked up her phone, and turned away from me while she spoke. Five minutes later, a round-faced woman about my age stepped off the elevator and walked straight to the reception desk. She wore a light blue blouse, sleeves rolled to the elbows, and black polyester slacks. She blew curls of faded red bangs off her forehead and smiled. The receptionist introduced her as the city editor.

"So, you're here about the pervert?" She laughed, and nodded for me to follow her.

We sat on a bench across the lobby, and I explained everything. I told her every last detail just as Peter had described. But the city editor said the paper was doing a story about the vice squad's crackdown on prostitution and its new approach of targeting the demand—the money-waving, dirty old bastards who come in from the suburbs, scoop up these poor girls, and do terrible things to their young bodies. Part of the police department's plan, she said, was to expose these men, to get their names in the crime reports, to shame the ones who got caught and scare off the others.

"Don't you think every single one of these guys says he deserves a break, that he's never done anything like this before?" she asked.

"Believe me, Pete is a good old soul." I looked her in the eyes, so she would know I wasn't messing with her. "He's mixed up. His wife's got one foot in the grave, and he can't stop wondering if he'll ever know what it feels like, if he'll ever get to experience this thing he's thought about all these years."

"Imagine that," the city editor said, "a lifetime without a hummer."

"Pete's just mixed up. He did a foolish thing."

"Jesus, did he ever. And then he went and told the truth about it."

I couldn't tell if she was making fun of Pete or if she was seeing my side. I didn't know how to make her understand the sadness and trouble her paper could bring to Pete, to Maryland, to all the people in our neighborhood who knew them and wanted only good for them.

"If you could just talk to the reporter," I said. "Just tell her the circumstances."

Two weeks ago, right in time for Christmas, the girls told me about their mother's boyfriend. I had taken them over to the Steak Inn for dinner, and while we waited for the food, my oldest said Mom and Travis had taken them to a Minneapolis hotel with a huge water park. When I asked who Travis was, my youngest said, *Mom's friend.*

I excused myself, walked to the hallway near the restrooms, and dialed Nan from the payphone. When she answered, I mumbled a hello and struggled over what to say next. She asked if something had gone wrong on the way to the restaurant.

"Travis," I said. "Why do I have to hear about Travis from the girls?"

She went quiet on the other end of the line.

"Who is he? Where did you meet him?"

"Look, Carl, I have my life now. You have yours. Don't make yourself a victim. I've already heard about your friend with the silver station wagon."

I had to think for a second. "A cleaning lady. The girl with the silver station wagon is a cleaning lady. She comes once a week."

Nan said nothing. I could hear her steady breath. I wondered which neighbors had been gossiping about my cleaning lady. No matter what they'd said, Nan must have seized on it as an excuse, a justification for her actions, a way to make her infidelity look like the direct result of something I had done or failed to do. I knew how that sort of thinking worked.

"If you wanted somebody else," I said, "you should have said so."

I rose early the next morning, dashed out into the cold before sunrise, swiped the newspaper off Pete's step, and scanned it in the light of our foyer. I did the same again the next day and the next. I did it until finally I saw the headline I'd been waiting for: Vice Cops Target Johns. The story topped the front page of the local news section. I skimmed the text for Pete's name, followed the jump to the inside page, and stopped at this paragraph:

Officers hear all kinds of excuses from offenders, from the predictable ("I was just giving her a ride") to the bizarre. An older man from suburban Falcon Heights claimed his late wife of four decades years had steadfastly refused to perform oral sex. He said pure curiosity prompted him to pay for the services he desired, but police interrupted before the transaction could be completed.

That was it—scant details, some of them wrong. I rolled up the paper, snapped its rubber band back in place, and sneaked across to return it to Pete's doorstep. As I retreated down the front walk, I heard the door creak.

Then the screen door opened and Linus pattered out at the end of his leash, with Pete trailing behind.

"Good morning, Carl," he said. "Anything good in the paper today?"

I shrugged.

"It's all right," he said. "I've been watching you all week. I appreciate your concern, but I'm not worried about it."

"Oh," I said. "Well, good, you shouldn't be."

Pete nodded and smiled. I waited for Linus and him at the curb. The dog turned and headed up the street, Pete followed, and I fell in beside him. We passed through the entire neighborhood that morning, up and down each block as the sun rose and warmed the air. What a sight we must have made—old Pete with his bushy eyebrows and wild hair poking out from his cap, me with icicles in my beard and flannel pajamas visible between the bottom of my parka and the top of my boots. We walked and walked that day, and all the time, we talked about the weather, our wives, and other things we didn't understand.

Watch Him Burn ❧

BRODIE SMITH

Frankie valli's biggest passion in life was the other frankie Valli, the famous one. Frankie had been born only a decade after the Famous Frankie Valli, in May of 1944, and so their common name was more kismet than anything else. He came from the same part of Newark as the FFV, the First Ward. It wasn't as much as a coincidence as it might seem. Valli was not all that uncommon a name for Italian immigrants. Frankie probably knew more Frankies than he had eaten hot meals in his life.

Of course Frankie knew that the FFV's given name was not Frankie Valli at all but instead Francis Stephen Castellucio. In some very real sense Frankie Valli's use of the name predated that of the FFV's, because the FFV did not adopt it as a stage name until some nine years after Frankie was born. Even the ineffectual assholes at the FFV fan club knew this kind of most basic trivia. For some eleven years, Frankie had been a dues-paying member of the FFV fan club, had struggled against the political sluggishness of the organization in what had amounted to an eight-year effort aimed towards getting the FFV his harrowingly overdue star on the Hollywood Walk of Fame. To be quite honest, Frankie did not understand how such a gross oversight could have been allowed to slip by for so long. He wasn't sure why you would even have a Walk of Fame if the FFV wasn't basically the ultimate star who all the other stars led up to, and he had been quite sure in the beginning that all it would really take was one letter informing them of this glaring omission that had probably slipped by because of his sheer obviousness. He really half-expected a letter in return telling him something along the lines of they conceived of the whole thing a sort of preemptive consecrative cenotaph or something, that God-forbid should something happen to the FFV, they would be ready to rechristen the entire place as the "Frankie Vallie Memoriam Hollywood Walk of Fame" immediately, so that a sum total of zero days pass without his life being honored. But it turned out this wasn't the case at all. They didn't feel that the FFV had enough "fan support" to qualify as of yet, a claim that Frankie personally found preposterous to the extreme, so much so that he was sure much more deviant forces were at work here, probably racism, not the typical 1950's Southern ilk but a much more heinous flavor, characteristic of the Biz in the 1970's, in which meritorious Italian-Americans, in this case an Italian-Americans *sans pareil*, were passed over in favor of lesser talents of Latin American or African heritage.

Evidentiary in such a claim, Frankie would always pull out what he considered the howitzer of Hollywood Walk of Fame reverse discrimination arguments, which was that in March of 1990, Tony Fucking Orlando had been given a star. Tony Fucking Orlando, a.k.a. the fucking Puerto Rican who ruined America circa 1970. Tony Fucking Orlando, who to this date had a two-show-a-night gig at Harrah's Hotel and Casino in Lake Tahoe, a job that should by all rights be the FFV's, since the FFV adores Tahoe and had always wanted to be steady at Harrah's. Tony Orlando, née Anthony Orlando Cassavitis, who owns and inhabits there a gigantic ranch-style mansion, named "Casa Tony," where he breeds and raises ostriches, a morsel of data which infuriated Frankie to no end, because seriously, what kind of ostentatious fucking Puerto Rican asshole raises goddamn ostriches on his multimillion dollar ranch-style property that he has the audacity to name after his Christian name alone. As if he is such a big shot that he preempts all other Tonys in the course of history. Only a morally depraved gluttonous fuck would raise ostriches on his ranch-style property for no other reason than he preferred his weekly omelets be made with ostrich yolks, since they had a meatier flavor.

Possibly the one thing that infuriated Frankie the most was that at "Casa Tony," TFO kept and bred a world-class show toy poodle who had won numerous dog shows as well as been runner-up twice at the Westminster Dog Show put on by the American Kennel Club each year in New York City. This is a poodle who, by all standards, Frankie would love to admire almost as much as he admired the FFV himself, because he found competitive dog showing to be a gravely overlooked art form in the contemporary world, in that it takes God's own handiwork and improves on it with human ingenuity and sense of contextual aesthetic value. Frankie found breeding to work much in the way that credible popular art like that of the FFV does, in that both start with an aggregate mass of stuff and then through a series of value filters manage to refine that normal stuff into something sublime. And he could even get past the fact that this particularly sublime toy poodle had such a devastatingly tasteless owner, because at that level of dog breeding, the owner had almost nothing to do with the breeding or training process, much in the way that owners of professional sports franchises have little or no say in the daily operation of their teams. No, the problem was that TFO had decided to name the poodle "Sherry," a moniker that Frankie knew was intended as a personal attack on the FFV himself (who was also particularly disposed towards poodles), making reference to the eponymous 1962 hit performed by the FFV as the lead singer in The Four Seasons, thereby making the whole act of christening the dog nothing more than a not-so-subtle reference to the FFV and TFO's own alleged "owning" of him. In other words, Frankie viewed the poodle's name as a comment on the FFV's current diminutive position in the popular eye vis-à-vis TFO himself. This simple dastardly act turned the poodle into a weapon of tyranny against its own will, for no matter how delicately crafted it is, no matter how inherently superior it has been made to others of its species, the act of creation is corrupted by impure motives. The analogy that Frankie liked to use was to the commonly retold myth of Helen of Troy, who was doomed to a destiny of strife no matter how pure a creation she herself was.

And the ineffectual assholes at the FFV fan club agreed with him, even if they were too cowardly or PC-whipped to admit to it. He and the fan club had parted ways after a lengthy and vigorous disagreement on how to handle the egregious Hollywood Walk of Fame situation. The fan club had wanted to reply either by (1) uniformly laying down and adopting a c'est la vie attitude, which the fan club justified with bucket loads of empty platitudes along the lines of "hey, we tried . . . it's their loss," and other bits of sophistry that do nothing but allow the shirking of responsibility, or (2) organizing some sort of pablum letter-writing campaign, as is designated SOP by the "official" Hollywood Chamber of Commerce website for stumping for stars, and which Frankie agreed with in principle as the correct methodology for proceeding in virtually any other case but this one, since they were talking

about the Fucking FFV here, not Perry Como or Jimmy Durante or
Annette Funicello or even Dean Martin, all of whom, incidentally, have
been included on the WOF. Nonetheless, Frankie swallowed his pride and
wrote a series of letters in 1983-1984, in which he systematically pointed out
the FFV's inherent superiority to performers who had already been given
WOF stars, citing extensive textual evidence in a concise objective manner.
For example, from the song "Grease," Frankie pointed to the lyrics

> *They think our love is just a growing pain*
> *Why don't they understand, it's just a crying shame*
> *Their lips are lying only real is real*
> *We stop the fight right now, we got to be what we feel*
> *Grease is the word*

which practically just bleed lyrical genius in that not only do they create
an almost overpowering urge in the listener to dance and sing along, but
they also successfully add a brilliant morpheme to American English by
associating with the signifier "grease: the idea of cutting through all the
establishment bullshit and "be[ing] what we feel," an idea that has reams of
implications that are too dense to unpack within the framework of a simple
fan letter (observe, for example, the textual knots drawn from even the simple line, "Grease is the time, is the place, is the motion," an idea that seems
to imply that grease is in fact not a hair product but rather a metastatic
entity that engulfs the Local and through some act of de-civilizing lubrica-
tion turns them into the Universal, or rather, reveals them for the Universal
that they already were), but that can be in essence boiled down to the act
of ignoring social convention and acting on pure human instinct, as if we
were unbound by the Freudian code of civilization that forces us to put our
own personal wants and needs behind those of the community at large, an
idea that is flawlessly summarized by the lyric, "only real is real," a turn of
phrase that is as epically gorgeous as Stein's "a rose is a rose is a rose," but also
encapsulates an entire aesthetic and political philosophy in a way of which
Stein could have never even dreamed.

But no matter how much analysis one does of the magnum opus, one can never really understand the glory that is the FFV without seeing him live and "be[ing] what you feel" in person, because the FFV has a stage presence that just demands emotional evolution on the spot. Along with the letters, Frankie mailed a series of envelopes containing videotapes of the FFV's performances, entitled "Watch him Burn," which, even though nothing like being there live, still portrays the absolute unparalleled skill with which the FFV can work a crowd into a frenzy with his body and skills with a microphone stand. But to each and every letter that he sent to the WOF Frankie only received in return a form letter stating that "[his] vote for [his] performer of choice has been registered by the Hollywood Walk of Fame and will be taken under consideration," which Frankie personally took very hard, in that it was like getting kicked in the stones by TFO three hundred and twelve times over the course of three and a half months and not being able to retaliate in any way whatsoever.

Frankie knew that he became a slightly different person after those three hundred and twelve letters. He was no stranger to effronteries. He had endured his share of hardships over the years. But those three months of rejection were his personal all-time low. Frankie took it as three hundred and twelve reasons why life did not answer to rational or moral discourse on any level, and instead relied on prejudice and the lowest common denominator of lazy and heartless entertainment. He tried his best to bear the burden like the FFV had done over all those many years that he had been refused the fame and fortune that he deserved possibly more than any other American in the course of the country's history, but this only made him realize that he was not the FFV, either in talent or moral fortitude, that maybe he was even a bad person, but that he was incapable of sitting there and taking it with a Christ-like smile of bliss while the Sorta Ricans and talentless, gutless sacks of rat droppings basically bent over himself and every other American with any trace of a sense of artistic and cultural value, and anally raped them while eating cooked dog meat and playing the fucking didgeridoo.

All of which goes a long way towards explaining Frankie's actions on the night of July Three, 1991, when he decided to turn the brunt of his aggression and lingering feelings of helplessness and betrayal at the hands of the Hollywood elite against one target in particular, the aforementioned runner-up in the Westminster Dog Show poodle category, one Sherry Orlando. Frankie had done his research. He had found that, as some sort of sick and twisted over-the-top megalomaniacal seasonal bonus, TFO had given tickets to all his staff to come see him perform at Harrah's on the big July Three show, which was the TFO's annual Superbowl-type gig because of TFO's blatant and base appeal to patriotism and in particular to "support our troops overseas." The upshot of all this was that Frankie knew that TFO's ranch style property "Casa Tony" was going to be completely deserted on that night, save one Sherry Orlando, perennial contender for BIS, who would be roaming the grounds at her particular whim without supervision.

Frankie gave a lot of thought to the situation. He considered whether murdering a poodle as a means of retribution towards the Hollywood elitist entertainment community and towards the lay public sentiment at large was, in fact, a sane thing to do. He considered what outsiders would think when they read the story in the paper or saw the ten-second sound bite on their local news—something along the lines of "Crazed Fan Murders Orlando's Dog As Retribution For Valli Snub"—and how pretty much everyone would just think of him as some psychopath stalker rather than as a true do-gooder, a balancer of injustices. In short, he knew that no one would get it. The act would not be successful as any sort of statement. In fact, it would probably further hurt the FFV's chance of ever getting his star, since his most famous fan would be a dog-murdering racist, a factoid that would have to reflect poorly on the FFV in the long run, this being more or less the prototypical counterexample to the well-known phrase, "all press is good press." It would not help the balance in the public sphere. But Frankie elected to proceed anyways, deciding in the end that karmic balance was more vital. Besides, he was just not capable of letting it slide.

And so on the night of July Three, 1991, Frankie made his way to the Orlando Residence in the outer suburbs of Lake Tahoe, Nevada, equipped with a 4-pack of BIC® lighters, a selection of old laundry that he knew he would never wear again, including but not limited to a 1989-1990 New York Knicks Atlantic Division Champions t-shirt and several pairs of shorts rendered useless by stretched elastic waists, along with six five-gallon cans of gasoline, to be used as an accelerant. He surveyed the house for several hours from a spruce tree in the backyard, watching Sherry Orlando make her way in a series of doggie doors that granted her access to various controlled areas of the grounds, until he was sure he had located all possible dog-accessible egresses from the interior of the estate. At 8:27 Frankie Valli made his way to the first doggie door and nailed a 2' x 4' board diagonally across it so as to prevent any exit. Over the next twenty-four minutes he did the same at four other dog-exits to the building, proceeding methodically, making sure that each was totally secure before moving on to the next. When he was done, he sat down on the back porch and waited precisely nine minutes until his watch read 9:00 on the nose, the designated time for TFO to begin his performance at Harrah's.

For those nine minutes Frankie regretted what he was about to do, regretted that it was necessary to resort to arson to avenge the two-decade-long snub that should be gnawing at the soul of every decent human being to occupy any above-ground real estate anywhere on the face of this kind and open-handed planet, a snub that was and would still be ongoing even after the prize poodle, Sherry Orlando, was long passed. But this was a serious conflict, and Sherry would be the first casualty of war. Her death would mark the beginning of the end of the free pass that the Hollywood elite had been enjoying for so long, would show them that there would be consequences for their idleness and immorality, consequences that, however small and meaningless, would remind them that they cannot unilaterally turn the key to artistry and culture at their own whim, that the people cannot and will not be manipulated indefinitely by vulgar Jews with six-figure convertibles and bad combovers. Frankie didn't really believe it but he told it all to himself anyways, told himself that the FFV mattered, that he mattered, that there was a moral compass, and that there was, for everything and everyone, a reckoning.

He flicked the lighter and set it to a pair of ratty old boxers, dropped them onto an incendiary trail of gasoline that ran twenty yards across TFO's impeccably manicured lawn, the kind that Frankie had always dreamt of holding tea parties on with his own daughter on Sunday afternoons, the kind that the FFV deserved, the kind all great and caring and thoughtful human beings deserved. And the flames larked across it, like water running downhill, like the way carpets unroll in cartoons, quickly painting the bushes with light, coruscating upwards along the gasoline he had spilled all over the siding, grabbing ahold of the leaves in the gutters and then the shingles, all within a matter of seconds.

Frankie didn't see it. He didn't stay to watch. He took no pleasure in burning down this man's house. It was all just a necessary evil, and he was evil's instrument of choice. Billows of acrid smoke clouded his way out of the cozy neighborhood, and he heard what might have been whelps from one prize show poodle, or might have just been his overactive imagination. He turned onto the bucolic pathway back to his car, rubbed his eyes, which were beginning to water from the smoke, and, humming "Sherry," split the scene.

The Chorus ❧

ERIN SOROS

Stillwater, British Columbia

THE SKY WAS BENDING TOWARD THE MOUNTAIN. JUNE STORMS STEAL HEAT and light and come on fast. A couple of men choked the last logs, and the rest of the hooking crew hurried with the rigging to get out of the clear cut before the thunder. When the rain started, it fell sharp as hail. Small rivers streaked down our faces. Water sucked cotton shirts to skin. Other than a few saplings, the left side of the ridge was plucked bare, and now water was sheeting the dirt. We were done for the day.

What you did, what we're sure you must have done, was flip the safety rap back too soon. The cable had been pulled taut from the bottom of the mountain to the top, the eye splice wrapped around a stump to keep the cable from snapping loose and pulling back downhill. And suddenly the eye was free. It whipped around in a circle thirty feet wide, a whir of metal, jaggers sticking out of the cable to catch your body in its arc.

Charlie. We heard no scream, just the crack of the line across your chest, then the snap and crash of branches. By the time we turned to look, you were gone. We dropped our tools. The skyline finally rested. It had dragged you three hundred feet, we'd heard the roots and stumps tearing through your body. We found your right leg spiked in the dirt as if someone had planted it there, the thigh bone split and sticking through the skin. Rain was already pooling in the gouge. Thorvald pulled the leg out of the dirt. The foot dragged like it was trying to walk. A hundred feet downhill we found your head still attached to your chest. Your face had been scratched off, the bones smashed into a fine spray so we couldn't tell the white from the red.

"Wife won't know him."

"No."

The foreman pulled out his notebook. Tight black letters inside the columns: job, date, location. Then he handed over the pen so we could sign off that we'd identified the body. *Charlie* was no name for an Eskimo, but we'd never asked about that. You'd been a hook tender twenty years.

June 28th, 1944. We all signed.

The logging camp was bright, or at least the cookhouse was bright, even at this hour, three a.m. The generator hummed steady against the encroaching evergreens. An oil lamp on the cookhouse porch cast a pale glow. The cook was up, the bullcook was up, slicing, sweeping. Rain spat mud on the stairs faster than the bullcook could sweep it away. Rain on the network of wooden sidewalks that ran through the center of the camp and branched off to link each building to the next. Together the buildings formed a horseshoe: cook-house at one end, and bunkhouses running down in two long lines. Each building was a cedar rectangle with a low pointed roof—plank walls thrown up in a day—and small windows covered inside by drying shirts.

The commissary was off to the left, behind the cookhouse. It was dark yet, shelves glinting in half-light: toothpaste, shaving cream, tobacco tins. First aid supplies were crammed in the corner, a desk in the back for the timekeeper. He was still asleep, curled in a metal cot beside the foreman's, dreaming he was anywhere but here. Holding him in bed were the red, yellow and green stripes of Hudson Bay blankets. He'd bought the white sheets himself. And the throw rug on the floor, a stack of Western novels tidy against the whitewashed walls. Drops of rain spattered the beer bottles that lined the sidewalk by the cookhouse. In the bunkhouses the wooden bunks ran end to end with lousy heads. We slept two or three to a bed, on mattresses flattened and mottled with stains. No sheets or pillows. Mattress buttons digging into our backs.

Tonight, those of us who found you, Charlie, were lying with our eyes on the rafters, head cradled in hands, or we curled on our side to watch the rise and fall of the next man's shoulder. It felt good, the warmth of a bunk-mate's body. Breathe in, breathe out. Through the bunkhouse walls the rain released the wet pink scent of cedar.

The next morning the skyline still lay on the ground. We walked over it the way children avoid cracks in the sidewalk. Soon the steam donkey would drag it down the hill, a thousand feet of steel cable, and we'd be done with it. We'd be able to walk away from this quarter, the logs gone. But the guylines and the strawlines were still rigged taut. We'd need to release those before we could get out of here, and that would be a good hour's work. Thorvald would sub for you. A new man would arrive in a week. A hook tender was never hard to replace.

The skyline we didn't want to touch. Not that we feared it. The line couldn't hurt a man now that it wasn't rigged tight from the stump to the spar. It lay on the ground lazy as a snake that's eaten its kill.

We've all held a man's photograph after he's gone, sad to see his smile that we'd never see again, or the way the scar on his brow sat like an umbrella for his eye. We've run our fingers along his cold forehead like we never did when he was alive. And we've touched their shirts like we touched yours, we've packed shirts and canvas pants and woolen socks and thought of the days and nights that wore them, good shoes, the shoes we never saw in the camp, shoes for walking on city streets, with city girls. What man can say he hasn't held those things? But this was different. This was no letter we found in a pocket and thought we shouldn't read.

Your body was still here though we'd done our best to remove it, bits of your skin and blood caught on the cragged rocks and stumps. A strand of hair like grass. The sun drying your blood until it turned to dirt, until the rains come down to make your blood run again.

We wanted to leave this hill. Enough of the fallen trees and the fresh stumps, enough of our caulk boots poking wet earth. Leave this hill alone and let the skyline rest.

Spruce two hundred feet high and eighteen feet thick, the hill crowded and dark with branches and underbrush we had to fight back to reach the next quarter, no space now to be thinking about a logger who wasn't here. It was Thorvald's job to rig the spar tree. His rope belt circled the tree, the Douglas fir soaring straight into a sky that was blank but for a belt of cloud. We stepped safe away and watched him lean back against the rope, watched him ram his spurs into the wood and limb the tree on his way up, sawing off the branches so they fell and crashed, the sound of them cracking as he walked to the top.

You were dead eighteen hours. We were back at work.

No priest for the funeral, no write-up in the *Powell River Dispatch*, no mothers from the mill town making pies for the widow. You were an Eskimo and a logger. When you were alive you rode with the Indians in the listing heat of the ship's boiler room while we sat above and played cards. You sat with the Indians in the balcony in our mill town's proud theatre—*first cinema in the dominion!*—where we went on special occasions to watch Indians killed. But you died in pieces and so your eulogy would come in pieces, in the torn bits of belief and conjecture blown from camp C to camp B to camp D, floating like burnt paper in the dark.

We were not religious men. Our woods housed no church. The only bibles we encountered were tucked in the night tables of Vancouver hotel rooms, small black witnesses to the white skin of women we paid. Each month we returned prodigal to these Doug Firs that dwarfed sin. What God was here? There was no watching presence in this thick green grave. When a man fell, the trees did not mourn.

We would bury you on Monday. Today was Sunday, day of haircuts. Day of moonshine and poker and rubbing our yellow-stained shirts against soap-slick rocks in the creek. Day when men crouched in their bunks to ink letters—those of us who could write and who still had a lady somewhere who remembered our real names. We licked the envelopes and imagined our tongues in other places. We never wrote of the men who died or how blood made us fear for our own crushable flesh.

Dawn came without you. Breakfast and lunch came without you. We were used to walking the camp on the days following a death, when a logger had been struck down by a branch or crushed by a rolling trunk. We were used to seeing him, the faller or bucker or boom-man, or thinking we saw him, sitting in his bunk or his chair in the cookhouse as if his body wanted its damn Sunday after its last week of work. The mind does not let go of the shapes it expects to find, so we knew that these bodies we saw were not ghosts or restless souls but our own hopeful vision, the way the brim of a hat holds the head more noticeably after the hat has fallen off.

Slack-jawed, sand-eyed, we drank our coffee. There's a sharpness to the air when a man hasn't slept the night or has slept it poorly, nerves electric on his skin—his mind slow while his legs are ready to run. In the brittle light we startled at the blue jays darting our hands as we reached for a smoke, jumped at the clang of pots and pans in the cookhouse, pulled away from the raw stringent stink of ammonia poured into buckets to wipe the floor clean. Even if we snuck back into the bunkhouse after breakfast for a Sunday nap, you would not let us sleep.

"I'm dead tired," Jackpot said. Heads heavy we leaned forward to feel the razor carve away this week's hair. The soap woke us. We sat on wooden chairs on the wooden sidewalk, the chair legs tilting uneven so that we had to brace ourselves to keep our necks steady against the blade. There was no barber, just the bunkmates who would want the same. We slumped, offered our necks. Four men sitting and four men cutting, reciprocal trust. Thumbs rough on the red tender skin. The hair fell into the sidewalk cracks. Then we stood up, sheep-shorn, our necks still wreathed in soap. We shook our bristled heads, new to the morning, and switched places.

Under our feet were the rolling papers that got caught in the same storm you did. They were still wet, torn by our boots and by the chair legs we tried to keep from wobbling back and forth. We could see through the paper to the wood of the sidewalk. If we picked it up, the soggy mass would disintegrate in our hands.

A bear walked through the camp, the bottom of his coat matted with dried mud. He was just a black bear, already fat on the spring's berries. Uninterested in us. We stood beside our wooden chairs and let him pass. The musky warm breath of bear. He sniffed the door of the cookhouse, sniffed a beer bottle left on the porch. Then he sniffed the bunkhouse windows, pawing the glass, and we knew it was our rank undershirts he wanted, the smell like the stench of his fur. He moved along. His shoulders rolled as he lumbered close to the ground. And this seemed a less vulnerable way to walk, using both the front legs and the back, not standing like one of us on two caulk boots as if we needed the sharp pegs in our soles just to keep us nailed upright, our heads high, bodies waiting for a tree to strike us down.

Charlie, on the job you spoke only when something was wrong—*Tight the line! Slack the sky!*—and so we remembered that you had yelled out, when you died. As the skyline dragged you downhill you shouted your last command. But that was just the line. It was the line that screamed.

You borrowed nothing. Drove up to camp with your own boots, your own ax, your own Swedish fiddle. Your death slipped through the camp without debt. The foreman ticked off your name in a book, wrote the balance of the upcoming paycheck out to your widow, and no one was sent to circle through the cookhouse calling out what you owed the company store.

In the days after your death, it was our own bodies we feared. Scar tissue does not move as easily as the skin surrounding it. Thirst could wake us in the dark to our own stinking parched breath. We wanted to escape this flesh that needs to be washed and watered and fed. We hated the fragile openings of the eyes, the joints that ached in our boots, rubbing blistered against the leather to let us know that this tough skin we needed for our protection was not our own. Repelled by our own smell, we escaped the bunkhouse only to be caught by the reek of piss, creosote, old beer. We sat down in the cookhouse where the slab of meat on our plate was too raw. The cook dropped a sack of sugar heavy as a man's chest.

Alive, we touched our leather suspenders, our plates, the rough edge of a cookhouse bench, all the solid objects that told us we had not been torn to bits. We chewed tobacco and hucked the black splats on the sidewalks and when it was our turn on Sunday again we tipped back on our wooden chairs to feel the fresh coolness of our hair being cut. The chairs creaking under human weight.

Then we took a second sandwich, more tobacco, another nap so we could fall dumb into sleep that tempted us with the sweaty grunting rutting we wanted most of all. Against death we wanted a woman's skin to suck and rub and enter. We reached for her, and the dirty sheets caught the rush of our juice.

The Report

NAOMI WILLIAMS

Samoa, 1787

WE HAULED THE WOUNDED ABOARD THE FRIGATES—THE *ASTROLABE* FIRST, then the *Boussole*. We kept our men from shooting the natives. We frightened off the canoes. We counted the men who returned from the cove alive. There were forty-nine. We counted again. Forty-nine. Then our commander, Mr. La Pérouse, had me follow him to his stateroom, and asked that I write a report on what happened. He said to do it right away while my memories were fresh. I reminded him that Mr. Boutin is senior to me. You oversaw the retreat, the commander said. But sir, I protested, Mr. Boutin has experience writing this kind of report. It was the wrong thing to say, a reminder of last year's calamity. The commander drew his eyebrows together and said, his voice low, Vaujuas, Mr. Boutin is *injured.* And then I felt like an ass, for how could I have forgotten? I'd hauled him up the side myself, held him when he staggered on the deck.

Mr. La Pérouse toyed with a marble bust on his desk. He has two—one of Rousseau and the other of Captain Cook. He fingered the base of Rousseau as if he might chip away at the stone. Any more questions? he asked. I left him, but at the stateroom door I looked back and saw him leaning his head against the fingertips of both hands, as if he were holding his skull together.

I was rowed back to the *Astrolabe.*

For two years I've wanted more quiet, but now I would give anything to go back to the din of yesterday. It was peace I wanted, not silence.

I will write the report tomorrow.

A boat came from the *Boussole* this morning with a parcel for me. It was a copy of Mr. Boutin's report from last summer, with a note from the commander: *Model your report after this one. Simply begin at the beginning and continue to the point when you returned to the frigates.* He signed his name Laperouse—one word, no accent mark, the L oversized and generous. I heard once that La Pérouse was not the commander's original name, that his family had appended the name when he joined the navy, to make him sound more aristocratic. The signature was that of a man unimpressed by such things and undistracted by minutiae. Undistracted by grief, I am tempted to say, but then I remember the way he held his head in his hands.

Begin at the beginning, he says. Is that half past twelve, when the four boats left the *Astrolabe* for the cove? Or one o'clock, when we landed at the beach? Or later, when I found some shade, and sat down alone, away from the others? Or later still, when the first rock was thrown? Or perhaps earlier, that morning, when our own captain, Mr. de Langle, invited me to join the outing? A walk on dry land will complete your recovery, he said. Perhaps *that* is where the story begins—a month ago, when our descent into this tropical heat left so many of us ill. Mr. de Langle was a great believer in the benefits of fresh air, clean water, and *terra firma.* He invited the convalescents on both frigates to join his watering expedition. That is how little danger he foresaw. I am not sure how many of us set out. Between sixty and seventy. I'll need an official count for the report. Sixty to seventy Frenchmen, but ten to twenty of us ill—off-duty, unarmed, ambulatory but not strong. This did not help our odds when the crisis came.

Come with us, Vaujuas, Mr. de Langle said that morning. I could have replied, Thank you, captain, but I have duties on board today, or Thank you, captain, but I still feel too unwell to leave the ship. But I did not decline. I said, Thank you, captain, I believe I will join you. He said, Maybe a pretty islander will bring you a coconut.

Today, tacking in front of the cove, we could see our wrecked longboats on the beach. They looked like the remains of an old skirmish, not yesterday's, of an encounter gone wrong between the islanders and some other explorers, not us. Amazingly, five or six native canoes came out to trade breadfruit and pigs with us. Did yesterday's catastrophe mean nothing to them? The *Boussole* finally fired one of its guns. The cannonball splashed right in their midst without hitting them, no doubt exactly as the commander ordered. One canoe capsized but was quickly righted again, and the natives hurried back to the shore.

※

Mr. Monty is now acting captain of the *Astrolabe*. He has always had the stooped shoulders of a young man surprised by growing suddenly tall, but now he also wears the pinched expression of a man who finds his ambitions fulfilled in a way he cannot possibly enjoy. This evening he asked how I fared with my report for the commander. I said I was studying Mr. Boutin's report from last year's incident in Alaska, so I should know how it was done. That seemed to satisfy him. He patted my shoulder as he left, trying out a gesture of Mr. de Langle's, but we both flinched and he drew away. When he left, I took up Boutin's report, which begins like this:

On July 13 at 5:50 a.m. I left the Boussole *in the small boat; my orders were to follow Mr. Descures.*

How difficult can this be? I take up my pen, and at the top of a clean sheet of paper I write:

Tuesday, December 11th

But I cannot tell how to go on. I was not on duty yesterday. I had no orders to follow.

※

Three days later, and the men are starting to talk again. I wish they would not. They stand in knots of two and three, considering aloud some detail they remember or have learned of the disaster. Even the Chinese sailors we took on in Manila huddle together on deck, and though I cannot understand their unlovely tongue, I know what they are talking about from the way they look at me when I pass. Thank God I am still officially on sick leave, which gives me license to avoid people.

Unfortunately, I still need to fix the number of men who were at the cove, and this requires conversation. It is awkward: I was the most senior of the *Astrolabe*'s officers to survive that day, but I was not on duty. That distinction belongs to Pierre Gobien, the midshipman who joined our ship eight months ago, when we met up with the *Subtile* in the Philippines. He should have the figures I need; he would have overseen the loading of our two boats that day. I saw him this morning at breakfast, and he looked up at me with a quick, sad smile, expecting me to speak to him. I nodded back but said nothing. I saw in his face a first experience of real grief, a yearning to draw someone into his confidence, and I recoiled. I cannot play the consoler, not for this. So although we are shipmates, and I know Mr. de Langle would have disapproved, I write Gobien a note and leave it under his cabin door.

I have also sent a similar note to the *Boussole* for Mr. Boutin, asking for an accounting of who went on the expedition from his ship and who returned. I am told that although he's still recovering from his injuries, he insists on aiding me with the report. I am unsure whether to feel grateful or put upon by his interest. I wonder, uncharitably, if he believes he should be writing it instead. I wish to God he were.

Every night I dream I am climbing up the side of the *Boussole* with the dreadful news of what happened at the cove. Mr. Boutin is always with me, but falls overboard at the rail, or blood gushes from his mouth when he tries to speak, or most horribly, he points to me and says to the commander, This man fired the first shot. I am never able to defend myself, to say, No, I was one of the convalescents, I was not armed.

We have finally sailed away from the island. Mr. Monty says it is called Mahouna, but the men are calling it Massacre Island. I hope they are calling it Massacre Island still in a hundred years. Nine leagues away is another island that looks much the same. We are surrounded by canoes that look just like the canoes we scared off two days ago, canoes filled with breadfruit and bananas and natives who look just like the treacherous natives we left behind. Some of our men claimed to recognize a few of the murderers and were ready to open fire, but Mr. Monty has strict orders from the commander. We are not to fire upon anyone without cause, we are not to allow any natives on board, we are not to anchor till we reach Botany Bay. We trade by raising and lowering a canvas between the deck and the canoes. I saw one native who tried to scale the side of the *Boussole* get beaten back with a long oar and fall screaming into the sea—a sight and sound that filled me with horror and pleasure both.

This morning Pierre Gobien came in reply to my note. He knocked tentatively, and I could hear him breathing on the other side of my cabin door. But I kept very still and at length he leaned over to push a note under the door. The boyishness of his handwriting surprised me. Later, in a more practiced hand, a note from the *Boussole,* from Mr. Boutin. I copied out their figures in my notebook:

Set out from the Boussole:	*Losses, Boussole:*
1 longboat	*1 longboat*
1 small boat	*—*
13 water casks	*11 water casks*
28 men	*4 men*

Set out from the Astrolabe:	*Losses, Astrolabe:*
1 longboat	*1 longboat*
1 small boat	*—*
15 water casks	*14 water casks*
33 men	*7 men*

There is satisfaction in the making of lists and the doing of sums, a satisfaction that even tragedy cannot quite erase. The numbers impress on me both the enormity of our loss as well as our relative good fortune. Eleven good men gone, our last two longboats destroyed, days' worth of water storage lost—I wonder that the voyage can continue. On the other hand, it could have been worse, much worse. I remember the deafening hail of stones on the beach and am amazed any of us left the cove alive. We managed to hold onto the two small boats, and forty-nine of us lived. Forty-nine out of sixty-one. But wait—wait. Forty-nine and eleven add up to sixty. We left with sixty-one. We have counted someone twice. Or someone is missing.

Dead calm today. There is sweltering below decks and sunburn above. Mr. Monty, bending his tall frame into my cabin, asked again about the report. I told him I was still assembling all the pertinent facts. I did not mention the discrepancy in the numbers. He said, Bear in mind, Vaujuas, that Mr. La Pérouse will include his own account of events in his journal. Yes? I said, not understanding, and Mr. Monty said, A man's account always tends to exonerate him. But the commander wasn't even there, I said. Mr. Monty cocked his head. Vaujuas, he said, as if recalling me to sense. Vaujuas, he repeated, the commander authorized the expedition; he's undoubtedly wishing he had not. The commander hadn't liked the idea from the outset, he went on. He and Mr. de Langle, they'd argued about it the night before. The commander only relented after Mr. de Langle said it would be the commander's fault if scurvy broke out on the frigates for lack of fresh water. Were they angry? I asked, and Mr. Monty said, Oh, yes, voices were raised. You were there? I asked, and then he drew his head back and said well, no, he'd heard the story from an officer on the *Boussole*. He urged me to complete the report as soon as possible and left for his cabin. He still sleeps in his old cabin off the council room. He only uses Mr. de Langle's cabin on the poop deck during the day.

I have completed the first sentence of my report:

Tuesday, December 11ᵗʰ, at eleven o'clock in the morning, Mr. La Pérouse sent his longboat and his small boat, loaded with water casks, and with a detachment of soldiers, to form part of an expedition under the command of Mr. de Langle.

The humidity makes writing difficult. The ink grows viscous, the paper sticks to my hand.

I wrote an entire page of my report today and felt pleased by my progress until I reviewed my work and saw that all I'd done was describe four boats and sixty-one men—or sixty?—headed for a watering place in a cove three-quarters of a league from the frigates.

Was the tragedy already inevitable at that point?

The only thing I remember from the trip to the cove is the behavior of Mr. Lamanon, the *Boussole*'s physicist and mineralogist. He arrived that afternoon in the *Boussole*'s small boat, wearing a preposterous straw hat he'd purchased in Macao and his torso crisscrossed with the straps of his leather specimen pouches. When his boat pulled up alongside the *Astrolabe*, he clambered into our longboat, nearly toppling several crewmen in the process. He declined to help row and spent the trip complaining to Mr. de Langle about the commander's lack of sympathy for the *Boussole*'s scientists. He regretted very much that he'd not been assigned to the *Astrolabe*, with its more sympathetic captain. He regretted too that the commander had not come along today to see for himself how superior these natives were to most so-called civilized men. Mr. de Langle laughed. You forget, Mr. Lamanon, he said, that Mr. La Pérouse is not only my commanding officer, but one of my dearest friends. I know, Lamanon said, I swear I cannot account for it at all.

What I could never account for was Mr. de Langle's tolerance of Lamanon. The man complained so much the officers on the *Boussole* called him Mr. Lamentation. He would seize on any excuse to have himself rowed over to the *Astrolabe* for dinner with Mr. de Langle, and then would pontificate the evening away while the captain looked on with amused interest. One evening, after Lamanon had intruded on one of our officers-only dinners, Mr. de Langle laughed at our pique. Of course the man has no manners, he said. He's a genius, he has no time for manners. One day his journals will make our voyage famous, he added, and you'll all be claiming him as a friend.

We have sighted a large island. I asked Mr. Monty what island it was and he said he did not know. I'm not as well read in the travel journals as Mr. de Langle, he added. Later the men wanted to know if they could go ashore, but Mr. Monty said, No, the commander will not allow it. Why not? one crewman called back, and I swatted the back of the man's head. Show some respect, I cried. Mr. Monty's your captain now.

I am back on duty, my greatly accelerated recovery one strange outcome of the disaster. Perhaps some constant level of energy operates among us, so that when some of us fall others inherit their strength. I don't know whether to credit science or Providence for this. I do know there is comfort in the performance of the myriad duties of shipboard life. I am especially glad to resume the astronomical observations, which I've overseen for most of the voyage, our astronomer having proved too seasick to continue past Tenerife. I am pleased by the reliability of our chronometer, pleased by the smooth workings of our English sextant, pleased by the neatness of my own hand as I take down my readings of the sky.

I have thought about Mr. Lamanon, and what he said in the longboat about wishing the commander could be there to see how delightful the natives were. I remember now what he said next. He said, Look. He pointed aft and we saw scores of canoes following us into the cove. Mr. Lamanon smiled under his straw hat and said, See how their innocent curiosity draws them to us. And Mr. de Langle, who had the tiller, turned around and swore. I wish they wouldn't follow us, he said. He gave the order to pull in the sail as we were approaching the reef. There are too many of them, he said, then concentrated on steering us through the narrow channel into the cove.

Perhaps the disaster was simply a mathematical inevitability. Hundreds following us into the cove, hundreds already gathered on the beach when we arrived: I wonder now that we didn't take alarm and turn around. Especially when Mr. de Langle realized that the tide was out. The longboats touched bottom a musket-shot away from the beach. Why did we not turn around then? Why did no one realize that we'd have to wade waist-deep through the water to reach the shore? That our weapons would get wet? That the water casks would be heavy after filling and would weigh down the already grounded boats? Some of the natives on the beach threw branches out into the water at our approach, and Mr. Lamanon said it was a sign of friendship. Mr. de Langle said he was heartily glad to know it. But I think friendship may not be possible between three score and a thousand, even when some of the three score are armed with muskets.

I write: *When we went on our way, we saw with regret that a large number of canoes were following us and coming to the same cove.*

It is ten days since it happened. This morning Mr. Monty came to my cabin, and I began a rehearsed plea for more time for the report, but he raised a hand to silence me, then asked if I would mind conferring with him on a map of the cove.

The map covered the council-room table. Fine dots for sand, thick dots for forest, thin lines for elevation, x's for reef. If only I could complete my report by scratching about in this way. Mr. Monty said he had had to guess the extent of the reef. Of course, I said. He pointed to one spot on the map and said, I understand there was only the narrowest channel through the reef. I said, Yes, it complicated our retreat. I assured him the map was fine, better than fine; it conveyed everything: the shape of the shoreline, the reef-choked cove and its narrow entrance, the thin slip of beach, the watering place, the hills that had blocked the frigates' view of us.

Mr. Monty cleared his throat. We need to draw the boats in as well, he said, then quickly added, Mr. La Pérouse requested it. He opened his hand and held out two breadfruit seeds and two grains of rice. The seeds are the longboats, he said, and the rice—. The small boats, I said, taking the seeds from his palm. His hand was sweaty. I put one seed down on the map, just to the right of where the stream emptied into the cove. The longboat from the *Boussole*, I said. I set the *Astrolabe*'s longboat next to it, then lined the grains of rice under the longboats. I ran my finger down the vertical gap between the two sets of boats. Most of the men who managed to get between the longboats had scrambled to the safety of the small boats, even some who'd been struck in the head by rocks, like Mr. Boutin, who I dragged bleeding out of the water. The men who ended up on either side of the longboats, on the other hand. . . . How was it we failed to notice all the natives armed with clubs?

Excuse me, Vaujuas, Mr. Monty said, but which of the small boats is which? I pointed to the grain of rice on the right. This one is ours, I said. The one you commanded to safety, he said. Yes, I said, the one I brought back.

I dream Mr. de Langle follows me up the side of the *Boussole*. We stole their canoes and escaped! he cries in triumph to the commander, then turns to me and demands, What did you dump the water casks for, Vaujuas, you numbskull rat?

I've gone over and over the lists from Mr. Boutin and Pierre Gobien, and I still cannot reconcile the numbers: sixty-one men off the frigates, forty-nine returned, eleven dead. I write another note to Mr. Boutin and send it to the *Boussole* by small boat. I slip another note under Gobien's door.

For two days now I've written nothing. I tell myself I need to be sure of the numbers, but I suspect this is no more than an excuse. The crisis—I have not yet described it, and it looms before me like an impossible thing. I cannot get beyond this, the last line I wrote:

There were among the natives several women and young girls who offered themselves to us in the most indecent manner, and their advances were not universally rejected.

I only noticed the women because I was off-duty and not part of the line of men busy with the water casks. Light-headed from the heat and lingering illness, I sat down in the shade and hoped I would not be dashed in the head by a falling coconut. I wondered if such things ever occurred. Then I heard the laughter of women behind me and turned to watch as they lured a few of our crewmen into the forest. They disappeared into the undergrowth, but I could hear them well enough, the forced, lewd cries of the women and the men's pig-like grunting.

I leaned my head back and closed my eyes, and when I opened them I found an older native woman pushing a most reluctant girl toward me. I shook my head but reached into my satchel and handed a glass bead to the girl and the woman, who I supposed to be her mother. The woman began raising up the girl's skirt while the girl tried to get away, and I shook my head again, trying to explain through gestures that I was sick and unable to do more. I was sorry for it, indeed I was; the girl had lustrous black hair that fell like a silk curtain over her breasts. My spirit was willing, but the flesh was weak, as the apostle says, although I believe he meant it differently.

When the girl realized she would not have to go through with what had been expected of her, she smiled and ran off. But a few minutes later she returned with a friend, and I was obliged to give her a bead as well. And not ten minutes later three more girls appeared.

I'm mindful of what Mr. Monty said—how my account will stand next to the commander's. I remember too his story about the disagreement between the commander and Mr. de Langle the night before the watering expedition. I wonder what the commander has written in his journal. Would I write differently if I knew? Perhaps it does not matter what I write. I have been given an order, that is all. Completion is the thing.

I need say no more about the island women, but the beads I cannot ignore:

As we completed the filling of the water casks, the number of natives increased, and they became more troublesome. Mr. de Langle abandoned his plan to trade with them and gave the order to return to the boats. But first, and this, I believe, to be the primary cause of our misfortune, he gave beads to some of the chiefs. These gifts, distributed to five or six individuals, excited the discontent of all the others.

I dream I've climbed up the side of the *Boussole* with the completed report already in hand. Mr. La Pérouse reads it and says, I thought *you* had the beads. We *all* had beads, I tell him.

We left France with a million glass beads. They are not Venetian beads, nor even the finest French beads, but they are pretty, with smooth, milky surfaces—milky blue, milky green, milky white. They are supposed to help us establish friendly relations with the natives we meet.

Yesterday we sighted Traitors Island, and today we hove to outside a large bay on its west side. Why is it called Traitors Island? I asked, but Mr. Monty shrugged. When we get to Botany Bay, he said, I'm transferring to the *Boussole*. I was shocked, and for one dizzying moment I imagined myself captain of the *Astrolabe*, until Mr. Monty said, quite evenly, Mr. Clonard will be transferred here to assume command. Ah, I said, that makes sense, he is senior to you. And then I should have said, I'll miss you, sir, or it's been a pleasure to serve under you, sir, or almost anything at all, but I said nothing, and Mr. Monty said, It's time you finished that report of yours, Vaujuas, and walked away.

The natives of Traitors Island came out in their canoes and traded with us in good faith, apparently unaware of the name given them by a previous explorer. They did not have much, but we were able to procure coconuts, bananas, a few yams and grapefruit, a pig, and some hens. They liked the beads, but were also interested in our iron, which bespeaks a better breed of native, more practical and hardworking. Still, we never let down our guard and not one was allowed on board. One of our men noticed that nearly all of them had one or two joints of the little finger of their left hand cut off. We had not seen this before.

§

Tonight Mr. Monty and our scientists are having dinner on the *Boussole* with the commander and their scientists. I've assigned Pierre Gobien to the watch and now sit at the council-room table to work uninterrupted on the report. Reviewing the completed pages, I come to the point where I left off:

These gifts, distributed to five or six individuals, excited the discontent of all the others.

Somehow I must get from gift beads to rocks being thrown; from an orderly line of sailors to dozens of men flailing and screaming in the water; from a beach full of curious natives to a mob of deadly savages. I write:

There arose at that point a general murmur, and we were no longer able to control the islanders.

I fear this will not do, not at all. But from this point I can only remember my own actions, and I cannot, must not, write of myself. I could say that I stayed by Mr. de Langle as he tried to distribute the beads. That when he saw me, he shouted, What are you doing, Vaujuas? and ordered me back to the boats. That rushing across the beach and into the water, weaving my way through the natives, I felt a surge of panicked vitality that was the first sign I had of a return to health. That I saw that the *Astrolabe*'s small boat had no officer aboard, and decided to wade toward it. But no—this is not a personal account. It's a report about an encounter with natives:

Although they allowed us to return to our boats, one group of islanders followed us into the water, while others gathered stones from the shore.

Mr. Monty came back from dinner flushed with wine. I learned why it's called Traitors Island, he said. Schouten and Le Maire were attacked by the islanders here 150 years ago. It had to be something like that, I said. He had also learned about the islanders' strange habit of severing their fingertips. They cut them off to pray for an ailing friend or relative, or grieve a lost one, he said. I looked up from my report. You and I should have no fingers left at all, then, should we? I said. Mr. Monty smiled sadly. I am not sure Mr. La Pérouse will recover from this, he said. I looked down, remembering again my last sight of the commander in his cabin. He blames Lamanon, Mr. Monty went on. He says Lamanon's absurd ideas about the savages caused Mr. de Langle to let go his customary caution. I'm not sure that's what happened, I said. Mr. Monty strode to the doorway, as if suddenly aware that our informality with each other was no longer appropriate. Finish the report, Vaujuas, he said, then perhaps we can all learn what *did* happen. But a moment later he was back, embarrassed, an envelope in his hand. From Mr. Boutin, he said, handing it to me.

Thank you for asking after me, Vaujuas, Mr. Boutin wrote. *I have lost the last of my head bandages and only frighten everyone on board now with my partly shaved head. As I said in my first note, we lost four from the Boussole.* And then a list, very neat, in rank order, with names in full:

> *Jean-Honoré-Robert de Paul de Lamanon, scientist*
> *Pierre Talin, master-at-arms*
> *André Roth, fusilier*
> *Joseph Rais, soldier*

I dream I've climbed onto the deck of the *Boussole* with Mr. Lamanon's straw hat, which I present to Mr. La Pérouse. Mr. Lamanon's compliments, sir, I say, then pull from the hat a glass jar filled with pickled human fingers. He takes the jar from me and hurls it overboard, and after them the two marble busts from his stateroom. Rousseau and Cook sink like cannonballs into the water.

During the night Gobien slips his reply under my door:

I can account for only the seven I reported earlier.

There is nothing for it but to tour the frigates, question every company, account for every person. I leave my cabin with a lead pencil and a piece of paper, and begin at the poop deck, where I write:

Paul-Antoine de Fleuriot de Langle, captain

Who would have believed, before December 11th, that muskets and swivel guns were no match against rocks? But muskets must be understood to be feared, and they must be used to be understood. They must also be dry to be usable, and then must be reloaded, a difficult matter when you're wading through water, or in a pitching boat filled with bleeding and panicked sailors, or cowering under a hail of rocks.

Mr. de Langle was doomed by his moderation. He somehow made it back to our longboat and ordered the grapnel raised, but several of the islanders held the cablet to prevent our leaving. Instead of firing at them, Mr. de Langle fired in the air, which rather than frightening the natives worked like a signal for a general attack. If we hadn't been the intended target, we should have been most impressed by their surprising skill and strength in throwing rocks. Later I would think, guiltily and irresistibly, that had he survived, Mr. Lamanon would have found a perfect marriage of physics and mineralogy in calculating the velocities and trajectories of the natives' missiles.

Mr. de Langle was knocked over in the first volley, falling across our longboat's thwart and then into the water on the port side, where the natives set upon him with clubs. A similar fate awaited everyone who remained in the longboats. For every native that fell to a successfully discharged musket there seemed to be ten to take his place. I got the *Astrolabe*'s small boat to the reef, and looking back, saw that an officer from the *Boussole* had command of their small boat. We began dumping the water casks overboard to make room for the men who swam out to us. The last I saw of my captain, the natives had hauled his bloodied body out of the water and were tying one limp arm to a thole-pin on the *Boussole*'s longboat.

I go below decks to talk to the seamen. Don't forget my brother, a man growls from his hammock. I make my way toward him and ask him his name. Jean Hamon, he says. And your brother? Yves, he says. Why aren't you up, Mr. Hamon? I ask. My legs, he replies, they're swollen. I feel a chill at this revelation. I ask if the doctor is treating him. He doesn't answer. His friends, who've gathered around, tell me he figures it's judgment for what happened at the cove. What do you mean? I demand. The men look at one another, then one whispers, Well see, sir, some of us who were there, we became friendly with the women, and Jean here thinks we might've caused some unpleasantness that led to the fighting that killed his brother. Not one of you is to blame for what happened, do you hear me? I say. I point to one seaman: Go tell the surgeon about Hamon's legs. I ask the others, Who else did you lose down here? They crowd around, watching me write in the dim light.

Yves Hamon, sailor
Jean Nedellec, sailor
François Foret, sailor
Laurent Robin, sailor

I speak next to the chief gunner. He scowls. It's been nearly three weeks, he says, you're only now getting around to figuring out who's dead? Just tell me who you lost, I say. He walks away as I write:

Louis David, fusilier

I then make my way to the galley, where I find Mr. de Langle's suspiciously thin cook, Deveau, and Mr. de Langle's cabin boy, François. Deveau hears my errand and says, Of course you've counted our captain, God rest his soul, and François repeats, his voice breaking, God rest his soul. I suspect they've been drinking. What about the servants? I ask. Deveau says, There was poor Geraud, and François echoes, Poor, poor Geraud.

Jean Geraud, servant

With that I have the seven Gobien listed for me. Who else can there be? I wonder, shaking the list in my hand. François says, Sir, didn't we lose one of the Chinese out there? A Chinese? I say. Yes, a Chinese, Deveau says, nodding with approval at François before saying to me, You forgot about them, didn't you, sir?

I go up on deck and find Pierre Gobien. I have so successfully avoided seeing him that I am shocked by the large scab on his forehead and his still blackened eye. He'd been the last to leave our longboat alive. What is it, sir? he says, looking at the list in my hand. Is it possible, I ask, that one of the Chinese was killed in that cove? He clicks his tongue and draws in a long breath. Yes, he says, we did lose one of them, now that you mention it. Had he a name? I ask. No doubt he did, Gobien says, but I'm damned if I know it. I stare hard at him, and he adds, Sir. I complete my list as he walks away:

a Chinese

Next I find Mr. Monty. We may have scurvy aboard, I tell him. Then I return to the council room, where I am now, where I am prepared to stay till I've written my way through the disaster. I thought I'd only been pretending that the discrepancy in the numbers was an obstacle to completing the report, but the freedom I feel now is not imaginary. My mind is easier. The missing man was not even French.

It is nearly dawn before I finish describing our retreat from the cove and our arrival back at the frigates, and I am wondering again why the natives didn't massacre all of us. Their canoes were faster than our small boats under any conditions, much less laden as we were with forty-nine men, only a few of us uninjured enough to work the oars. They could easily have prevented our leaving the cove, but they didn't. We rowed back through the channel in the reef and only a few canoes followed us, heckling us but careful to keep a safe distance from our muskets, whose power they now understood.

When we came in sight of the frigates it was as though nothing had happened, as if we'd passed through a nightmare world and would now wake to the safety of our lives aboard the ships. Scores of canoes still surrounded the frigates, and we could see natives on deck visiting and trading with our people. No one on board even noticed us or our distress till we were quite close. We reached the *Astrolabe* first and delivered the injured, then made our way to the *Boussole*. Mr. Boutin and I fairly crawled up the side. At any moment I feared one or the other of us might faint and plunge into the sea. He was bleeding from the head and very pale. Later I would discover a gash on my own head, but whether the injury was caused by one of the native's rocks or sustained during our frantic escape, I cannot say.

Once on deck, Mr. Boutin saw the commander and cried out, We were attacked, then dropped to his knees. I tried to hold him up, but he's larger than I am, and dragged me to the deck with him. An angry cry came from the men, and they ran for their weapons—soldiers for muskets, gunners to their cannons. The commander stood in shocked silence for a moment, then cried out, No! Do not fire! Seeing one of the men grab a native on deck, he shouted to let him go, whereupon the frightened native leapt overboard and swam away, followed by the other natives on board. The commander took his trumpet and called over to the *Astrolabe:* Do not fire! I repeat, do not fire! He ordered the survivors brought up from the boats below, had Mr. Boutin taken to the sick bay, then turned to me and fixed my face between his hands. My God, he said, what happened? They killed him, I cried. Who? the commander said. The captain, I said, it was the beads, he was trying to help. The commander shook me. Where is Mr. de Langle? he shouted. He told me to go back to the boats, I said, so I did. Then the commander's face crumpled in grief. No, he said, no, not him, not like this, and I cannot say now whether he held me or I held him, and whether the sobs I heard were mine alone.

It is New Year's Day, 1788, and I have completed the report. Mr. Monty insisted I deliver it in person, so I put on my dress uniform and was rowed to the *Boussole*, the first time I'd left the *Astrolabe* since the disaster. Mr. Boutin, head bald in patches and hair cropped short elsewhere, greeted me at the deck with such warmth that I drew away. He saw my embarrassment and stepped back. Mr. La Pérouse is waiting for you below, he said, his voice low and formal.

There are few agonies worse than watching someone read your writing. I stood before the commander as he sat at his desk with my report, and I thought of a dozen sentences I would have rewritten. I also saw how the commander's uniform hung loose from his shoulders. At the beginning of the voyage, some of the younger officers and I had called him Commander La Paunch. It seems now like an ancient memory. At last the commander looked up and said, It's a good report, Vaujuas; you've been most fair to all concerned. I'd been holding my breath, and gasped out, Thank you, sir. I particularly appreciate the ending, he said, then read aloud: *Everyone who was there can attest, with me, that no violence or imprudence on our part preceded the savages' attack. Mr. de Langle had given us the strictest orders in this regard, and no one disobeyed them.* I thought it might be important to emphasize that, I said. You can scarcely imagine how important, the commander said, and the color rose in his face. Critics at home are always ready to blame the explorer when there's trouble with natives, he added.

Then he turned back several pages, and asked, Do you have any idea how many natives died? No, I replied, surprised. There were shots fired? he asked, and I nodded. He pressed: You must have seen natives fall during the battle; who suffered more losses? I shook my head. Proportionally, sir, I said, we did, of course, by far. But in total numbers, perhaps they did. I'd like to think we killed at least thirty or forty. But it's only a supposition. Should I have included that in the report?

The commander shook his head, dismissing the question; he'd turned again toward the end of my report, his mind already on something else. You lapse into eulogy here, he said. I said I wasn't aware of having done so. He read aloud: *As for me, I have lost a friend more than a commanding officer, a man who always showed a kindly interest in me. I will regret his loss forever.* He glanced up at me, eyebrow raised in question, and I felt my face flame as he read on: *If only I could have given him some mark of my attachment and regard by sacrificing myself for him.* Should I delete those lines, sir? I asked. No, the commander said, no, then remained silent for so long that I wondered if I should leave.

Do you remember the last thing Mr. de Langle said to you? he finally said. Yes sir, I said, he told me to go back to the boats. I mean before that, the commander said. He looked so expectantly at me and so dejected for himself, and I remembered that he and Mr. de Langle had argued the last time they saw each other. Yes, I said after a moment, yes, at the cove, he joined me for a time beneath a pine tree—. A *pine* tree? the commander asked. A *palm* tree, I corrected myself, then went on: Mr. de Langle turned to me and said, Take a good look, Vaujuas, remember everything—when we get back to Europe this will all seem a dream. The commander nodded mournfully, and I wanted to say, Sir, it's no use dwelling on the last words exchanged. But it was not my place to say so.

Mr. de Langle did join me once beneath a tree. He said everything I reported to the commander. But it wasn't at the cove on Massacre Island; it wasn't here in the South Seas at all; it wasn't last month or even last year. He said these words to me, but not on the day he died. It was over a year ago, and we were sitting on a point overlooking Monterey Bay, in California. Mr. Lamanon was arguing in Latin with one of the Spanish priests. Can you understand what they're saying, sir? I asked Mr. de Langle. I believe Mr. Lamanon is trying to persuade our host that there is no God, Mr. de Langle said, and when I frowned, he laughed. Take a good look around, Vaujuas, he said, Try to remember everything. I did as he bid. The fog was receding. Sea otters played in the water below us; stretching out into whiteness beyond was the great expanse of the Pacific. When we get back to Europe, Mr. de Langle added, this will all seem a dream.

It is already a dream.

Every night, before the always-changing dream of climbing up the side of the *Boussole*, I dream this prologue, which never changes: I'm under the coconut tree at the cove on Massacre Island. Native girls crowd around me, their brown fingers reaching for my pouch, calling out for beads. Word has spread, apparently, of a white man who will give you a bead for nothing. I get to my feet when they won't leave, and waver where I stand, lightheaded from hunger and fever. No more, I say to them, holding the pouch over my head, beyond their reach. One girl jumps up and snatches off my hat, and another grabs at my jacket, trying to twist off the buttons. Stop! I shout, trying to shake them off. I slap at one with my free arm and she jumps back with a cry into the arms of a naked, tattooed man who might be her father. He growls in my direction, at which several other native men come forward. An older woman appears and orders the girls away. They slink off, pouting and grumbling, sometimes stopping to shout back an insult. The men begin to circle me. *What are you doing, Vaujuas?* Mr. de Langle cries, leaving the watering line and advancing toward me. He grabs the pouch from my hand. *Get back to the boats!* I do as he bids, I hurry to the water's edge and walk in up to my knees, then turn back. He is trying to distribute what is left of my beads. I see our unattended launch, and plunge into the water after it.

Stricken

MARK WISNIEWSKI

My wife's name has changed at least four times. It was Elizabeth at birth, Betsy when I met her, Liz-Ann just before we married—and Beth when she fell out love with me, which might or might not have been my fault.

If you're struck by lightning, you have a decent chance to survive. And the odds say that most of your skin will appear untouched. Your wrist will redden if you were wearing a watch when hit; blisters will appear beneath any keys in your pockets. Almost certainly, you'll suffer hearing loss, at least for a time, as well as muscle spasms, coordination problems, attention deficits, and the inability to sit still. If your memory remains unaffected, doctors will consider you lucky.

One evening when my wife was Beth, I behaved idiotically. There are reasons for what I did, but they'd seem like excuses to the average person, and given the state of my memory, I mistrust myself when I think I was justified. What I do know is that, not long before this idiotic behavior, my wife kissed our brother-in-law Len as we arrived at her sister Karen's house. I'll admit it was a hello kiss, in that sense presumed innocuous, but it landed more on his mouth than his cheek, and it lingered, and her fingertips petted the stubble on his jaw as she ended it, as if to tell him or me or her sister Karen—or all of us, including her sister's two young sons, who stood behind me then— that she, Beth, was falling out of love with me. For my part, observation of that kiss seemed to pass through my eyes and no further, my thoughts and feelings about it arising in disparate wisps months later. In any case I'm sure that, despite my troubled memory now, a kiss of that sort did happen.

Maybe half an hour after that kiss, the obligatory initial conversation among the adults played itself out, and Karen and Beth (she was then most definitely Beth) and Len and I found ourselves playing hide-and-seek with my nephews Jeff and Hunter. Jeff was It first, which gave me a rules-sanctioned excuse to hide, which was all I wanted to do. In fact—or at least among the facts I remember—I even declined a beer Len offered in order to head straight for the unlit basement, tiptoeing down the stairs like a child, then rushed to what struck me as an excellent spot: the tub in the unfinished bathroom. Not long after I yanked closed the navy blue shower curtain, someone pulled it open halfway, and I shrunk back damning myself for having been found by Jeff so soon, but then Karen stepped into the tub and stood with her back to me.

A cloud need not be overhead for you to get hit. Certainly rain isn't necessary, though a rush of clouds and a downpour often preface the worst strikes. If a mountain, or even a hill, obscures your view of the sky, you face an increased risk.

I'll probably never know whether Karen saw me before she closed the curtain. In any event, her shoulders were now inches from my chest, warmth from her scalp rising against the underside of my chin. Her presence of course had me startled, though I also recall thinking our proximity had resulted somewhat naturally: we'd both hidden downstairs because we'd both seen the kiss and felt drawn toward descent. Then, in an attempt to get a laugh we might share with Beth and Len at dinner, I simultaneously covered her mouth with one hand and, with the other, clutched her waist. In my mind, the precise manner in which I did these two things has never changed. What changes is why I did them. Usually my memory assures me I wanted to scare her into humor yet not have her scream loudly enough for us to be found.

I've never told my wife what I've thought about her shifts from name to name. But at that point in our marriage—the year we visited Karen and Len in Missouri—the shifts she'd made irked me. Sometimes, often when I was alone, I'd worry that she was trying out names the way Karen was known to try on clothes during shopping sprees: capriciously, endlessly, insisting nothing fit perfectly. To me, each new name suggested that my wife, when she got down to it, didn't know who she was. What will happen, I'd think, when she does finally know? Will she care about me? Will she leave? If she never understands who she really is, how will I?

Karen didn't scream. Instead, she allowed herself to relax against me, pushing me against the tile wall. She giggled, and then she licked my palm, a gesture I took as payback for my hijinks or an awkward sexual advance. Either way, I liked her even less—she and I had never hit it off owing to her materialistic bent—but if this were her way of suggesting we kiss to even our scores with our spouses, my pride told me to indulge her. That's when I removed my hand from her mouth. And that's when she turned and faced me. And we did kiss: her lips just beyond the edges of mine, a greeting well beyond obligatory, a jilted lover's kiss, the kind you feel the need to prove you can continue well, with finesse.

Inattentiveness might be the worst result of all. It's not really inattentiveness, but that's how it appears to anyone close to you. You are, in fact, trying to concentrate on your surroundings, but the amount of information at hand exceeds your capacities, and you simply can't take it all in. The hum of an airplane and the sight of a wasp, on top of, say, your hatred of war and the reluctance of an elm leaf to follow the sweeps of your rake—these things together could overwhelm you to the extent that you find yourself watching the sky to revisit the starting point that, yes, a plane is flying overhead. And then: No, it is not a military plane. Often you will conceive of yourself as hyper-attentive, but the person close to you will see you as unfocused. Now and again you'll find that apparent peace between the two of you has burst into argument. If such an argument proceeds logically, you will lose, but you won't know that you have, or how. It is therefore crucial to your marriage that your spouse try harder to understand.

Maybe I don't need to detail what happened just after Karen and I kissed. Truth be told, I tend to remember those moments haphazardly. I conjure various moments well, but their chronology escapes me, as if, all these months later, my mind is trying to render them on the whole senseless and therefore impossible. There was Karen unbuttoning my shirt. There was me untucking her blouse. There were more giggles—hers, I often believe, though some very well could have been mine. There were more kisses, a number of them pecks bereft of emotion save perhaps the desire to buy time to consider our options. There was a deft unbuttoning of my trousers. There was the nick of a protruding nipple, and certainly hesitancy on my part that seemed to fuel her breathing. There were fears—disguised hopes?—that someone would discover us, and there were recurring thoughts of Beth kissing Len, thoughts that, at least then, I was sure Karen and I shared.

It's difficult to swallow just after you've been hit. For days afterward, you'll crave ice chips. Your libido will be reduced or, in effect, gone. If urges for sex return, they'll time themselves inconveniently. Often they'll manifest themselves quickly, then vanish, bolstering your confusion.

Whether or not Karen and I had a single thought in common, the curtain beside us opened about halfway, and Hunter said, Mom?—and I doubted he could see me for the darkness and the curtain, but I cringed: he must have noticed that Karen's blouse was undone.

You're not It, she told him. Are you?

Jeff already found me, he said. And I have to pee. Bad. Aunt Betsy is using the bathroom upstairs.

Aunt *Beth*, I thought, and Karen asked, You wanted to pee in the tub?

No, Hunter said. But I kept hearing noises.

That was just me, Karen said, and what happened after that generally fails me. I do remember that I buttoned my trousers confident that, yes, I'd remained hidden, and it also occurs to me now that, while I was otherwise gathering myself, Karen was smoothing things over with Hunter, who told her Jeff had found their Aunt Betsy first, meaning Beth would be It in the next round. I've always known that I waited behind that curtain, holding onto it, listening to Karen and Hunter discuss yellow cake as they walked upstairs to use the bathroom off the master bedroom, feeling relieved that I was again alone—but then, as I sensed that my marriage could end, I absent-mindedly pulled the curtain free from two of its plastic rings. I will never deny that, as I steadied myself against the cool tile wall, I feared the upstairs: feared this woman who, if you asked me then, was more of a Beth than she was my wife. Worse, I didn't want that woman to know who *I'd* become: a husband who'd crossed a line with his wife's sister for reasons healthier minds might have deemed petty.

In some respects, it won't matter whether you or your spouse was the actual victim: for both of you, the marriage will change fundamentally. If you're the one who was hit, you might not be able to work, so your spouse might need to take a second job, or change careers. And your spouse will sleep fitfully on the nights when you wake repeatedly. You will both become sleep-deprived and as a result irritated. If one of you suggests separate beds, the other might agree, in which case you'll both be reminded of how it felt to be single. And medical care can be an issue—if you can't work and your spouse is away from nine to five or longer. You might not need constant care, but common sense will suggest you not be left alone for long stretches.

Blame Karen, I thought as I stepped out of the tub. She did, I told myself, press her backside against me. And Beth had kissed Len too fondly, and no denial of that could stand as the truth. And I was, after all, human, and male at that: weren't men presumed unable to control themselves in the throes of insecurity and temptation?

And: I had hesitated. Pretty much all I did, I thought then, was hesitate. Hesitation shows commitment, I thought. Doesn't it?

Then I heard, I see you! And there, in the bathroom doorway, stood Jeff, all five years' worth of him, pointing at the man he'd needed to find before he could hide from his aunt in the second round of our game. Wait a *minute*, he said. Hunter told me my mom was in the bathtub. You were hiding in there too?

Yes, but only for a little while, I said.

Two people can't hide in the same place, he said.

Why not?

That's the *rule.*

Since when?

Since my dad said so, he said. Dad, isn't that the rule? he shouted as he ran upstairs.

Isn't what the rule? I heard Len call, and the door to the basement closed, presumably at the hand of Len, who would now, no doubt, learn that his wife and brother-in-law had hidden together in the tub in his dark basement. I wasn't sure, as I failed to decipher the ensuing conversation, if I'd been tucking in my shirt when Jeff had discovered me, but my shirttail still hung over my belt. I tucked it in, wiped my lips hard with the backs of both hands, then paced the length of a cinder block wall. Across the basement was a refrigerator, the largely abandoned kind couples with children tend to stock with soft drinks and a six-pack for old times' sake. I bolted toward it, opened it, twisted a can of lite free from its plastic collar, shouldered the door closed as a chill hissed against my finger.

I sipped hungrily, then walked upstairs. There was Len, making a fruit salad beside the kitchen sink. He didn't as much as turn my way as I strode past him for the living room, where the eyes of Jeff and Karen and Hunter shifted to me as Beth, with her hands over her face, began to count out loud: her stint as It had begun. Karen shot me a look that confirmed everyone knew we'd been in the tub, then dashed upstairs so quickly I wondered if she needed to compose herself privately—or was she suggesting I join her? The boys were now also gone, down a hallway that led to rooms I'd never seen. I sipped more beer, Beth's count at twenty-six. I had no idea how high she needed to go, no desire to play. I returned to the kitchen, where Len nodded at the table and said, Try under there. No one ever looks there.

Listen, Len, I said.

She's on forty-one, he said. Better get under there. Or somewhere.

But I want to talk to you, I said.

About what? he asked.

What happened downstairs.

So you took yourself a cold one. That's what they're for.

I'm not talking about the beer, I said.

Then Beth called out: Fifty!

Now or never, Len said, and I ducked under the table, spilling foam onto the thigh of my khakis. I was crouched uncomfortably, my neck resisting my head's desire to rise despite the underside of the table. I was half of a silence shared with Len—until I heard Beth's high heels.

I'm not playing, he told her.

I know, she said, and soon, from the sound of things, she was gone.

Just after a strike, sleep escapes you. Months down the road, though, you and your spouse might sleep as many as fifteen hours straight. Of course the physical body needs to recover, but either of you—or both—might now be depressed. Even if you were blissful before you were hit, you can find your-selves feeling doomed. And if either of you suspected infidelity before the strike, you risk wallowing yourselves into trouble.

Game's over, dude, Len said, and I had every intention of facing him and the boys and Karen immediately, but the proximity of the table to my head and the effects of middle age on my knees—along with, perhaps, a pair of shock-stiffened shoulders—had frozen me. It was as if I'd hidden in a broom closet and someone had locked and leaned against the door: that's the nature of the claustrophobia I felt, if only briefly. Then, after a few grunts intended to explain my delay, I maneuvered myself out and stood eye-to-eye with Len.

You were right, I told him. No one looks there.

Yeah, he said. You just gotta know where to go. He stepped toward the fruit salad, and, wiping his hands on a paper towel, seemed to frown, though he did appear to be swallowing quickly, as if he'd just sneaked a mouthful. Karen! he yelled toward the living room.

Yeah? she called.

Get the boys' butts in their chairs!

We're eating now? I asked him, and he left the kitchen, passing Beth as she walked in.

There you are, she said. She glanced at my thigh.

That's beer, I said.

I guess you'll always be hopeless, she said—and Karen shouted, Betsy? Time to eat!

Can you believe it? Beth asked as I followed her to the dining room. After all these years, she still calls me Betsy.

Sometimes I still fatigue easily, and I still fear thunderstorms. Many times these days, I consider only what happens to cross my path. For example: Do butterflies know where they're going? Do they distinguish one flower from the next?

Dinner offered the interruptions children naturally bring, the kinds that don't allow adults to converse in linear fashion, and for those interruptions, I was grateful. At the same time, I knew what was happening: the kisses my wife and I had shared with our in-laws were being distanced from us by time, food, drink, and the needs of the boys. In that sense, those kisses were now more difficult to discuss than they would have been had I allowed myself to be found first while Beth was It.

I could have crouched beside Len's recliner in the living room so she could have found me just after she'd reached fifty. I could have told her, in whispers, that Karen followed me into the tub and came on to me, and everything could have been over.

But I hadn't allowed myself to be found. I'd hidden. In order to win.

At the boys' request, Beth, Len, Karen, and I—and the boys themselves—took our slices of frosted yellow cake to the rec room, to watch *Saving Private Ryan* on Len's large-screen TV. The carnage was as graphic as I'd remembered it, far more so than that in *Apocalypse Now*, and I wondered, while we watched and ate and then merely watched, how startling the newest war movie thirty years from then would be, as well as how tame *Ryan* would seem to the boys after they had aged into their forties. Would both of them marry? I thought. Would either cheat or be cheated on? How long would Hunter be able to picture Karen, standing flustered, as exactly what he'd seen before he learned that I'd been in the tub with her? Would Jeff always remember that his mother had been with me when she broke the rules of the game? Was the sight of war all anyone needed to forget certain horrors of love?

Confusion can feel like a friend after you've been hit. It was bonded to you when you returned to consciousness, and then it remained with you, always at your side as you recovered. It followed or led where you walked. It wanted to hang out regardless of your spouse's moods. There was tightness there, between you and confusion.

Len clicked off the video, *Private Ryan*'s credits be damned. Sack time, boys, he said quietly.

That goes for me, too, Karen added through a yawn, and I was sure Beth believed that she and I were on the verge of a war of our own.

What you and your spouse will want to keep secret are the seizures. They are, of course, hideous. They might not happen until weeks after the strike. The first one, while it occurs, might scare your spouse more than you. Probably one of you, and then finally both, will suspect epilepsy before you are told otherwise. EEG's don't access the parts of the brain short-circuited by lightning, so you'll be told you've experienced a *pseudo*seizure, and you'll be advised not to worry, to soldier forth, to trust that such episodes, like most aberrations of the human body, will pass.

As Beth and I left Karen and Len standing just outside their front doorway, I was sure Beth and I faced a decision: either mention our kisses as soon as we closed ourselves inside our car, or agree implicitly, by silence, that we preferred not to discuss kisses of any kind: that only children need concern themselves with strict expectations, that for all practical purposes, our day was done. And after both of our doors were closed, we did fall into a silence. I never imagined then that, months later, I'd wish we'd spoken our minds. In our car then, a kind of wisdom suggested we let our separate thoughts take us into the night.

It happened after the brown rice was boiled for dinner, after Karen had called and talked to Beth and Beth had strolled into the kitchen and hung up the phone. I was beyond casual hunger, so I halfheartedly asked, What's the word?

Len filed for divorce, Beth said.

Oh, was all I could say. Then: Shit.

She's upset, of course, Beth said. I mean—naturally. Though not as upset as you might think.

When did he file? I asked.

Two weeks ago.

What were his grounds?

Infidelity.

His or hers? I said, a half-assed joke to hasten us toward eating.

You can probably imagine, she said.

What's that supposed to mean?

She just told me. About you and her. In the tub.

I'm sorry?

In the tub. In their basement. When we visited last year. The details are in the divorce papers, in case your memory needs refreshing. She told me because she wanted me to learn everything from her first.

Another man might have lost his appetite right then, but I didn't. In fact, as those moments passed, hunger ate at me.

Hey, I said. We didn't fool around. I mean, it was mostly just a kiss.

That's not what she said. And at least she apologized right away. That is, after she admitted it.

Well, I don't know what she admitted to. I mean, who knows *what* those divorce papers say. But I apologize for the kiss, if that's what you want. But since we're all suddenly being so up-front about that night, *I'd* like an apology—for that gooey kiss you planted on Len. Which, I might add, happened before Karen came on to me.

Now she *came on* to you?

When did I say she didn't?

I thought it was mostly a kiss.

Whatever it was, it was no worse than what you did to provoke it.

Don't go trying to put this on me, Tom.

Why not? You did what you did, in plain view of me and everyone there, including those kids. You show off like that—the great kisser—and people notice. In this case those people included your sister and your husband, who, whether you like it or not, had feelings.

That doesn't mean they go fuck in a tub.

I walked from the stove to my side of the kitchen table, then back to the stove. This is stupid, I thought. No, I told myself. *You* were stupid. But that doesn't mean you need to take all the blame.

I turned around and said, We didn't fuck, Beth.

But you didn't just kiss.

I was clutching the sides of the stove, the rice fattened, ready to burn.

Yes, I said. I suppose we didn't.

You *suppose?*

To be honest, I said, I don't remember it exactly. Which is, as you know, understandable. I was really thrown by how you kissed Len—

For Christ's *sake*, Tom. She's my *sister.*

And Len is my brother-in-law.

I don't think I've ever even *pecked* Len.

Now that's a goddamned lie, I said, and I headed straight for her, two stiff fingers aimed at her as if one, and she flinched as if she thought I'd hit her, so I pivoted, left the kitchen for the hallway, and walked into the mud room, where I told myself that hunger had gotten the best of me. But if you accept blame just to *eat*, I thought—and I swung at the wall with a punch that missed, then flung open the screen door and dashed to the far corner of the back yard, stopping only because of our chainlink. I heard thunder but saw no lightning, but then a bolt did appear, only the top of it visible, most of it hidden by trees on the rise behind the chainlink itself. It was then that Beth appeared at the side of the house, marched nearly all the way to me, and pointed at the sky. As I remember, I shrugged callously, and she said, But there's lightning, and I said, I don't care, and she said, Just come inside with me, and I turned and huffed off, at first to underscore that I was on my own way in, then on the assumption that I was leading as we made our ways separately. Out of that wistfulness that rises when you're freshly ticked off but already wishing you weren't, I looked over my shoulder, now hoping she'd join me, now worried about her safety, and I saw her standing more or less where I'd been, near the chainlink, glancing up, as I had, after the sound of more thunder, and that's when it struck. It was thick, so oddly wide that I knew only respect for it, respect I now believe I needed to cling to as I absorbed the truth that she was down, stricken, lying on grass, eyes closed, hands open, fingers curled. Her heart wasn't working when I got to her, but in some number of moments it was, no thanks to me in the sense that I had yet to attend to it directly, maybe, I now often hope, thanks instead simply to my presence: it was my hand squeezing her wrist. I doubt I will ever be able to both remember and focus enough to explain everything that goes through you when you feel your wife's pulse begin again, on its own, as if the worst off-chances in nature, the ones that allowed her to be hit by lightning in the first place, also allowed her to survive what by all appearances should have killed her. You know she has changed. You accept that she is now aged beyond her years. You understand all at once the superfluousness of the human kiss, the inexactitude of names.

Christmas in the Neighborhood 🦐

CHRISTINA YU

For unknown reasons—perhaps it was global warming or just plain freakishness, my thirteenth Christmas was warmer than usual. Through November, the outside world retained its summery pigmentation, the afternoon a silver haze, and the dusk a sky of melting wax, oozing into purple as if a fierce candle had been held up behind it. Rain lashed the trees frequently, and everything came up greener and greener after each storm. As my parents, grandma, and I played mah jong late into the night, as we often did that winter, all the old summer sounds and scents prevailed—the creak of swing sets, the shrill presence of invisible creatures, the smell of tar and cut grass. When I lay in a block of sunlight on the pistachio carpet of my living room, the outside seemed like a mere extension of the domestic world within, changeless as the yellow walls and mahogany furniture.

In the pleasant weather, the families of my neighborhood brought their decorating to new heights. They inflated giant Santas on their yards, choked their trees in rainbow lights, and lined their driveways with chin-high candy-canes that swirled in continuous motion like slender, curved barber poles. It was the year of the inflatable snowglobe, and spheres of falling winter made their appearance on every street, as did elf automatons and talking reindeer. As December drew near, a few families hid movie projectors behind plastic rocks and displayed slide show scenes of snowmen and shifting snow flurries on the sides of their homes, transforming them into primitive, outdoor theaters. Why, we wondered, had the snow ever been necessary? Or the excuse of a holiday? It was as if the weather had freed us, encouraged us to take our decorating as far as we could imagine. The Jordans, who always had a towering Christmas tree shining out of each of their large French windows, decorated a fourth tree on their lawn, and dressed it as if it were an inside tree. An electric angel was set on top, and the branches were striped in gold lights and dripping with glowing neon bulbs in purple, red, green, and blue. To accompany this display, a row of red felt stockings were hung from the roof of the porch, suggesting that the Jordans had decided to shift their inside decorations outside this year. Taking their inspiration from the showy Jordans, the clever, subversive Thompsons moved their outside decorations inside. As we drove by, I would rub my hand on the frosted glass and peer out into the Thompson house which was always dark and pulsing with thin strips, like marquee lights. As we drove further away, it often looked like a cave of jewels, a loaded mine in the blackness, and I was sometimes seized with a mad desire to penetrate the home and lay my eyes on its secret illuminations. "So much trouble!" my mother remarked once, gazing out her kitchen window at the inside-out and outside-in decorating, hands busy in the sink. "And you have to take it all down. Might as well never put it up."

I, on the other hand, admired the Jordans. They held garage sales often, coordinated the neighborhood Halloween parade, and put up a white tent on their lawn every summer and threw a graduation or sweet sixteen party. We were never invited, but this was not their fault; we had never returned their dinner invitation from several years ago and had refused an offer to play doubles tennis once in the primordial past. Worst of all, we despised their dog which had long ago bitten my father on the ankle during a jogging trip around the neighborhood. It was because of this dog and its peers that my parents belonged to the gym at the Jewish Community Center. While I did my homework by lamplight after dinner, I often watched the Jordans walk their dog, the mother bouncing out the door in her red fleece and matching headband, dog zigzagging on its leash before the speed-walking couple. Sometimes their middle daughter, Josie, came out wearing jeans and a puff-sleeved peasant shirt. Her waistless, tubby figure never seemed to match her tight, angular face, with its mature profile. Each time I saw her, the fat seemed redistributed on her body, as if the folds, too, had come from a variety accessory pack. Once by the bus stop, I had been startled to see her up close (jaw cracking with gum, dimples appearing and disappearing), for I knew her as a series of unconnected images: head crooked over a phone, right arm wrapped around the waist and silver baton twirling overhead. Although Josie did not appear to have a boyfriend of her own, she sometimes took a stroll in the evening with an ever-changing clump of friends. As they moved together (a hackey sack or the red star of a cigarette floating between them), the boys would place and remove their hands from the small of the girls' backs, while the taller and fuller girls remained stiff, trying to minimize their stature beside the small boys. That winter-summer, they would linger outside, invisible like the trees until they passed by the projectors, returning to the Jordans' home—where I imagined they sat on tall, tall barstools swinging their legs and drinking fizzling beers from the loins of the refrigerator. Every evening, while my mother, father, sister, and I sat in the kitchen eating dinner, glasses fogging up with winter melon soup, I would watch Josie and her pals from inside until I felt my body rise from itself like a ghost and drift through the screen door.

I was not the only restless one.

"This year," my father began one night. "We are all of us going back to China for the Christmas break."

My sister placed both elbows on the table. "I'll go if you promise to subscribe to the alternative energy source for heating . . . Don't give me those conspiratorial looks—I just don't think you understand we're in crisis mode as a universe. Look outside, look at how . . . disgusting it is outside. It's completely unnatural."

My father nodded. "It is your mother and my fault that we did not install the habit every year."

My sister gave us all a smug look—*See!*

"Too expensive," my mother said, picking her teeth with a toothpick. "We can't just *dong bu.dong jiu hui.qu.*" *Get up and go for no reason.*

"It's only twenty dollars extra per month!" my sister cried. "As an upper middle class family in this country, we have a duty."

"Why can't we stay here?" I asked. "Why can't we just have a normal, stay-at-home Christmas like they do in the movies?"

"Bourgeois," my sister hissed.

"If you go, each of you girls can have an extra three hundred dollars," my father said.

My sister stabbed a fish ball with her chopstick. "To pay for the new heating service?"

Nobody answered.

"I'm going to the JCC now," my mother said. "Anyone who wants to come is welcome." Picking at her teeth with one hand, she rose to shut the mini-blinds.

Like some kind of domestic obstacle course, our hallway was littered with drifting plastic bags and unpaired shoes. Mother paused there for a moment to fold her towels and tuck them into the vinyl tote bag she used for exercise. Then we clunked down the garage steps and squeezed out between the cars. The night beyond the clattering garage door was thickly black and blinking with insects. As we inched down the driveway and wound out of our neighborhood, I glimpsed Josie and her friends at the far end of the street, their forms outlined in glowing jewelry, which upon closer glance, appeared to be necklaces and bracelets of tiny Christmas lights. The light was leaking all over them in a soft neon. We drew closer, and the group parted, eyes on both sides going dead for a moment, though I continued to stare out at them, unashamed of my interest. Out of the corner of my eye, I saw my mother's hand dart for the center of the steering wheel, and I pulled it away.

"I know those kids from school," I whispered.

"Don't they have homework?"

Over the next week, I noted from my bedroom window that the trend had caught on all over the neighborhood. Glowing espadrille-straps criss-crossed up the calves, chokers flickered around the necks, and fiery earrings exploded like tiny firecrackers above the shoulders. Hairstyles, too, came under the influence of the craze. After it became common for young girls to braid lights into their hair, the youngest Jordan girl appeared wearing a beehive hairstyle that contained a giant bulb inside, transforming her hair into a dim lamp. Nothing was more fashionable than the bulb that winter, and many of the high school girls were seen wearing "bulb pendants"—large, ordinary-looking bulbs placed snugly between the breasts. Most provocative, however, were the "x-ray" bras which were glowing bustiers worn beneath white or nearly transparent clothing. Because these items were deemed inappropriate for children under sixteen, mothers allowed their younger daughters to wear fist-sized hearts inside their clothes instead. These were placed over the heart to represent the organ in illuminated terms.

It did not occur to me that we were part of a national trend until I heard it discussed on the local news one morning: "Seasonal retailers are reporting an exponential growth in the sale of ornaments. What's new this year? Wearable lighting displays and solar-powered circuits that require no batteries. Concerned about safety hazards? Join us later with Donna Stewart . . ." At the school store that day at lunch, I noticed glowing plastic hearts for sale beside the novelty erasers at the cash register. "Magical Shining Heart" it read in bubble-letters on the pink cardboard box. I was already short with lunch money for the week, but I remembered that I had won a certificate the previous year for placing first in the science bee. Balancing my tray on a shelf, I dug through my lint-slimed pockets for the slip, then slid it across the table at the PTO mom who barely looked up from her novel. I placed the brown paper bag next to my glasses case in the front pocket of my backpack and for the rest of the day, carried it around on my back instead of shoving it into my slim locker.

But that night it rained and Father decided to make an announcement at the dinner table.

"I reserved four tickets for us. Excellent deal. Round trip to Shanghai."

"You can't just do that without consulting everyone," Mother said.

"It's just a reservation. We'll think about it and decide within a week."

My sister folded half her book behind the spine and let her eyes rest on the page as she spoke. "Count me out. I already signed up for a school-sponsored trip to build a house in Mexico for the people there."

"Do you have to pay for that?" Mother asked.

"Of course you have to pay for it."

"Anyway, just think about it," Father said. "I'll need to know by next Monday."

By the first of December, the homes had taken their projection displays a step further and turned them into full-blown outside movie theaters, the screens two or three stories high and interrupted by windows and balconies, where a robed housewife sometimes appeared, breaking the image and smiling down at the neighborhood guests like a queen before her subjects. At times, it almost looked as if she had emerged from the screen itself, a two-dimensional figure come to life. Indeed there was often a theatrical aspect to these outdoor scenes—a sense of deliberate order in the suburban architecture of the neighborhood, a sense that our surroundings had been designed for a grand performance of which we were all spectators. The first few days, the films were limited to black and white silent features, and only a few chairs and tables were put outside on the lawn for the family and potential guests. But within a week of the first film, each home began to feel like a public establishment, a café almost, and as many as five card tables and twenty fold-out chairs were seen outside on a single property. As more families purchased the projectors and recent releases began to appear in color, the tables were draped in cloth, the chairs padded, and details like vases and candles added to improve the atmosphere. At the Lowrys, one evening, the musical children performed on the piccolo during intermission, and soon after, spotlights were fixed overhead in the canopy to provide the establishment with an intimate, cabaret feeling.

As if he was spurred on by the rising excitement in the neighborhood or subconsciously afraid that we might become seduced by the fervor, Father pressed ahead with his plan.

"Tomorrow, I'm going to go ahead and buy the tickets," he announced.

"Just because we haven't responded doesn't mean we agree," my sister said.

"Nobody agrees," my mother said. "Anyone who wants to go can go by himself."

"Why don't we split up?" I asked. "The three of you go. I'm staying home alone."

They turned and looked at me. "What do you want to stay here for? What's here?"

"Well, I'm going to Mexico," my sister said. "Mom can go with Dad."

"I'm not going without the kids," Mother said. "What is the point? We're old."

"Bali," Father added. "What if we add Bali or Singapore? Would you girls be more interested? How about a halfway stop in Hawaii?"

"I'd go to the Far East with my own friends," said my sister. "But it's no fun with you guys. We've done it a zillion times, and it's always the same. There's no element of discovery."

"It's supposed to be the same," I whispered. "He wants it to be a habit, something we do every year."

"Girls too old for habits," Mother said succinctly. "They have to study for the SATs."

"It will be educational," Father persisted. "Mary, don't you believe in a global education?"

"I have a very high standard for what I consider educational."

Mother nodded. "Mary isn't interested in shopping for curtains or buying jewelry. She wants to be absorbed in native life."

My sister shook her head. "I don't do the tourist thing anymore. Or the family visit thing."

I had finished my homework early and gone out under the pretense of checking mail—only to be startled by the first notes. Perhaps it was because I had begun to see everything in luminous terms, but I experienced the music as drops of light, each note a glowing bulb in my consciousness, so that I felt the emptiness of my own black, silent yard with more intensity than before. With the mail under my arm, I considered going back inside where my mother was no doubt chopping onions and throwing a rainbow into the wok. But I could already feel the mah jong tiles between my fingers, hear the ticking clock and TV hum. I wanted the rippling piccolo instead. I had not come out into the night for years, not since I was a kid. Never such a thorough experience of the air, its trills of coolness, and scents of tire and dirt, whole mixture as singular and unrepeatable as a perfume. As I drew up a neighboring driveway, closer to the music and crowd, I noticed the Jordan girls sitting at a table on the edge. Their faces, as usual, were striped in moonlight. Instead of a puff-sleeved peasant shirt, Josie wore a soccer costume, suggesting that she had just come from a game. A chair was empty, so I sat down beside her.

She turned and looked me up and down. "It wouldn't hurt to ask."

For a second, I thought I had imagined her voice.

"I'm joking." She jabbed me in the ribs with odd familiarity.

"Have we met?" I bit my lip. The question sounded all wrong.

She rolled her eyes. "You're only my neighbor."

"That's right," I said. "A long time ago, you invited us to play tennis."

I bit my lip. That was stupid, too. Of course she wouldn't remember.

But she kept her eyes on the piccolo player and did not appear surprised at the question. "Yeah, why didn't you come?"

"I don't know."

For five minutes, we sat in silence, the music encasing us. I did not move, for fear I would break the moment.

"Tomorrow night, we're playing softball. You should come."

"Where?"

I did not play baseball—I despised balls—my father and I had never stood outside on the lawn playing catch like other children and their dads.

"Outside, silly."

"I'll be there," I mumbled.

During that epoch, it was not uncommon for families to linger with popcorn and candy in the driveway cafés of the outside theaters, children spilling out into the road with baseballs and bats. Though I studied them carefully from my window, I could never quite grasp the contours of the games. They were always shifting up and down the street and morphing into increasingly unrecognizable games that made me recall the spirit of rainy Saturday afternoons and impossible, made-up board games with multiple spinners, hourglasses and buzzers, and segmented pathways that intersected each other so many times it was impossible to find the end. Always, there had been two sides: those who pressed for more and more complicated games, and those who preferred conventional games whose pleasures lay not in the proliferation of accessories but in the elegant simplicity of rules themselves. Now that the games occupied the road, the driveway, and the lawn, it was possible to follow the evolution of evening athletics from any window, and watch how some children drove the games into good-natured chaos by crossing boundaries and performing choreographed victory dances that sparked the losers to steal their caps and flags. At the height of these games, the neighborhood became a giant stadium, each living room a box seat at the show. My favorite game involved a huddle, followed by a chant, and then a mad scattering to the distant corners of the neighborhood as a red kickball was launched into the air, high above the trees. The rules of this game eluded me, but I loved to watch the dancing lights of the sneakers which created altogether the image of a slowly expanding explosion of light, a firework that spread across the ground. As the dusk deepened, the effect grew more startling, and I saw only the lights themselves from my window. At around nine o'clock every night, as if the children were afraid of pushing their games too far, the sneaker-lights, would disappear one by one.

As I slipped out the door for my first baseball game, wearing the only pair of athletic shorts I owned, I felt as if I were walking into the empyrean.

From across the street, Josie put her hands on her hips. "Well, look who we have here."

The other Jordans and their friends turned to stare at me with curious eyes.

"What are you waiting for? Toss me that!"

At my feet lay a ball. I bent down to pick it up and for a moment stood with my arm back, not knowing what to do. Then I closed my eyes and threw it as I had always imagined.

It curved and landed in Josie's palm—as if she had thrown it herself or drawn it toward her like a magnet.

"Shall we begin?" she cried with mock formality. "Me and the neighbor against the rest of you, okay?" As she spoke, she strode toward me and locked her arm in mine as if we had been best friends forever.

Nobody laughed at me as I stood over the towel-rag base.

"Keep your eye on the ball," Josie whispered from behind, as her sister Marisa smirked at me. "I don't think you can handle this!"

"Throw em the old Uncle Charlie!" I heard from the sidelines.

Tightness constricted my chest. The ball came toward me, I swung, and for a second, thought I had missed it.

And then I was running, running for my life under the stars, *in* the stars, a mad glee bubbling in my veins. As I slid into second base, I shot Josie a grin. No one seemed to notice that I looked awkward in my tight-necked and oversized crew T-shirt that covered my shorts.

"We-want-a-pitcher, not-a-belly-itcher!" someone cried.

The night, it seemed, was alive with joyful shouting: "Awww, come on! That was wayyyyy outside!" and then "Kill the umpire!" and "Just make contact, man. Just go for contact. That's all we're expecting!"

As the game progressed, it grew more chaotic. The towel-rag bases grew rumpled on the road and were kicked into the grass. We ran, we slid, we leapt, we went after each other, and tumbled in the lawns, squealing and fighting over the ball.

I did not know how much time had passed before Josie nudged me. "I gotta go in." And then over her shoulder: "See you tomorrow night."

Back at home, Mother was standing in the kitchen over the sink, contorting her face as she tried to unscrew the top of a kimchee jar. In the orange glare of the kitchen, I was both disappointed and relieved to see my familiar textbooks, the old wok, Father snoring on the sofa in the living room, a China guidebook splayed across his belly.

". . . I'm going to write a letter to this company," Mother was saying. "Tell them to make their tops less tight."

"Please don't do that."

She shot me an indignant look. "Remember when I complained about the hotel toilet? I got us free complimentary breakfast."

She slapped across the tiles in her house slippers. "I'm going to burn this off."

No, I would never tell her about the softball game.

"The trip to China?" I asked instead. "I'm assuming Dad finally gave up on that?"

"You can ask him. Last thing I heard, he extended the reservation."

❦

After the success of the piccolo performance came a series of performance acts throughout the neighborhood: harmonica bands, baton twirling, poetry recitations, and lectures from high school students who wished to inform the public about social issues. And with these acts came the microphone and speaker cords, the music stands and podiums, the applause, the crowds, the captivated silences. Why, after so many years of calm, were the nights filled with music and drama now? Perhaps it had all come about because the lighting displays encouraged a certain level of showiness that naturally evolved into live performance. I had no words to describe it then, but the era was like all periods of strange effervescence that flare up for no good reason, then taper back into ordinary life.

One thing was certain: what had begun as a good-natured rivalry between the Jordans and the Thompsons, what was initially mere excess brought on by the pleasant weather, had now evolved into an epoch of community involvement. Anything could be a theater, we realized: a basketball court, a driveway, a living room, even the road itself. One week after the first piccolo performance, a group of kids from the high school theater club staged a scene from *Hamlet* in the back of a truck. This act was followed by another truck carrying a pianist who sat with his back exposed to the sky while his hands lay deep within the lacquered box of an upright piano. The piece was a nameless tune from a nameless book of technical exercises, but the show inaugurated a series of "performance parades" that marked the transition from spontaneous driveway performances to the Golden Age of Performance. By the tenth of December, the MacKenzie girls had begun to rehearse ballet scenes from *The Nutcracker* and later that week, we were treated to a midnight performance of the Arabian Dance on their driveway. Though I could not hear the music as I squinted from my upstairs window, it seemed to come from within me as the girls slithered and contorted themselves, folding and caressing the air. For some reason, they did not wear costumes, only rolled-up jeans and ballet shoes. It was as if they might break into their jerky school movements any second, and I watched with breath held, hoping they would not. After the triumph, Oscar Wilde's *Salome* soon opened in the garage of the Masons at the top of the hill, and featured the first adults to perform in the neighborhood. Using binoculars from my window, I could make out the crinkled newsprint of a peacock skirt and the explosion of red ribbon (from a shirt pocket), which I took to signify blood and guts in the suicide scene.

In all this, my greatest desire was that Josie and I might perform together, that we would fall into a rhythm of rehearsals, that she would invite me to sit with her on the counter in her kitchen and . . .

❦

"I gave it up. The tickets are gone," Father announced at dinner one evening.

"Good," Mother said.

"Why?" my sister asked.

"It's apparent that no one in the family is interested in staying connected to the home country."

"So I cancelled my trip to Mexico for nothing!" my sister grumbled.

My father shook his head. "The best deal ever. We'll never find a better one. It's really a pity."

"Don't look at me," my sister said. "I'm the one who made real sacrifices. I cancelled my own trip and gave up the deposit."

"I never cared either way," said Mother. "I was fine with everything."

They looked at me.

"Okay," I said. "I'm sorry. It's all my fault."

"You don't mean it," my sister said.

"I mean it," I said.

Among those who came out into the night, there were several surprising appearances. The wiry Thompson twins appeared on Fridays, dressed in suspenders, striped shirts, and red berets, selling drinks and cartons of nuts and popcorn. I watched from my window as they sauntered up and down the driveway, responding to calls and balancing the silver snack trays on their forearms and palms like proud waiters of some fabulous restaurant. Sometimes I caught sight of their faces, which were whitened with powder and blackened around the eyes as if they were mimes or actors in a silent film. As I watched them from my window, I forgot that I rode with them on the school bus, that they often joined me in the front seats, our noses stuck in books—that once, long ago in elementary school, we had skipped gym class together in order to avoid the nightmare of picking teams.

Because there was such an audience for the lawn displays, they grew more outrageous as the winter deepened and the temperature refused to drop. This, after all, was the year of walnut and berry-sized lights, bird and dragonfly shaped lights, trellises of grape lights, icicle and stalactite lights, fiber optic waterfall lights, and ice lights which could be placed within and beneath ice sculptures and sheets of fake snow to provide the neighborhood minimalists with lawns of textured light, of dramatic shadow and radiance. In this spirit of variation, the spectrum of colors grew more expansive and subtle, with as many as fifty shades of green in a single outfit: a blue-tinged sea foam, a blinding chartreuse, a translucent cobalt, an acidic lime, a deep malachite, and a dim, whitish jade. This was the year of colored glass and mineral blends, of mosaic bulbs, and bulbs that were crusted in jewels and given as gifts to lovers. Resembling chocolate boxes and printed in futuristic and antique colors, the tins in which these lights came packaged were a hit in themselves and later came to represent the era in the same way that hatboxes evoke their own century. Some were even padded like purses and lined inside with shocking pink or green satin. Today, reproductions of vintage advertise-ments can be purchased in the city museum, though the boxes and bulbs themselves are collector's items that fetch a high price in auctions.

In our own neighborhood, the High Age of Decorating came the second week of December. The MacKenzies, for instance, stretched hun-dreds of blue Christmas lights across their lawn, then strung glowing green lily pads across the blue stripes to create the appearance of a pond. They completed the effect with a human-sized frog that sat upon a brown log at the edge of the yard, beaming its liquid eyes and exuding a texture of slip-pery froggishness that had been achieved with the exacting use of all fifty shades of green. As we stepped closer, we noticed the warty lips, the pale underside of the legs and belly, and the poisonous black and blue spots along the hindquarters. The display was a triumph of decorating, the frog realized in astonishing detail and the impression of water evoked so realistically that some hiked up their skirts before stepping into the tangled sea of lights. A day later, hundreds of thin silver laundry lines appeared in the front yard of the Lowrys, so that it appeared to be an enormous spiderweb in the daytime. All afternoon as I worked on my problem set, I could not help but glance over at the Lowrys' yard, hoping to catch the mysterious transformation, the moment when the lights would illuminate, the evening fade into darkness and the meaning of the lines revealed at last. As usual, the transformation, the most conspicuous transformation in all the world (it happened every night, all over the world) eluded me. In the orange light of my desk lamp, I bent my head for too long, and raised it to find that the lines had become invisible. Instead, I saw three, glowing magic carpets suspended in the blackness, each six inches thick and displaying tassels and intricate designs all over the surface. For a second, I blinked. For a second, flying carpets *did* exist, and I knew that if I raised my eyes even further, I would see the tiny silhouette of a carpet-rider moving across the push-lamp of the moon. The next evening, a head-sized Jupiter with gaseous rings appeared above the carpets and a black sun flamed near the porch, which was kept dark, as was the rest of the house to give the display full effect. Thus began a new school of decorating in our neighborhood, that which ignored the framework provided by the house and sought to create in spite of existing structures.

In contrast to these eccentric folk, the cul-de-sac at the end of the street I lived on was inhabited by traditionalists. In the fashion of other, less-evolved neighborhoods, they kept their decorations a hodge-podge of typical Christmas images—Santa Clauses, reindeer, and snowmen, and refused to be restrained by a single cohesive theme, unlike the MacKenzies who had chosen pond-life and the Lowrys with their celestial objects. These families relied mostly on department stores and supermarkets for their decorations, and though I preferred the Lowrys' eccentricity, I was grateful, too, for the simplicity these families provided in that outrageous period. Though each property could be placed somewhere along the spectrum between experimental and traditional, some properties aimed for neither category. These families decorated their homes with orange, green, and blue rope lights that made the homes look as if they had been outlined by some cartoonish hand.

The effect was a home whose shutters and windows looked as if they had been drawn by a childish giant. The jolly Robertsons belonged to this simple school of decorating. They highlighted the contours of the bushes and trees in blue rope light and hung a blue "BAR" sign and a neon yellow martini glass (filled with green liquid and rimmed with pink) on the front of their home. For some reason beyond me, those who practiced this school of decorating often incorporated signs that read "CAFÉ," "NO SMOKING," and "NO SOLICITING" into their displays, as if they longed to bring the public life into their homes, create an urban atmosphere in our sprinkler-twitching streets. Popular beverages, clothing labels, brand logos, sports teams, and barbecue condiments were also illuminated in similar fashion.

Then there were homes which fell into no school and whose displays were not copied by any neighbors. The woody backyard of the McCulloughs, for instance, was lit with thousands of tiny pale orange lights, so that from far away, it looked like a raging forest fire. The effect was so powerful that the fire department was called by a passerby from the highway side of the property. In the absence of winter, the season was evoked on the lawn of the Kents through white snow-lights which came not in strings but clumps of varying density—the denser the whiter. To enhance shadow, tiny blue and black bulbs were thrown in with the white. These were attached to the branches to create frost and heaped on the lawn to produce snow. For those who could not decide which school of decorating they most admired, it became fashionable to decorate the property to accommodate many different themes and illuminate only one set of lights at once, so that multiple, overlapping scenes could flash across the yard in a single minute.

For a week, I saw nothing of Josie. I could not say what exactly I wanted. Another baseball game? And if so, how many after that? And what purpose would they serve? I had been taught not to hope for anything, to expect nothing of people. But as long as the lights burned every night, anything was possible.

"It's your lucky day," Father began one night at dinner.

No one said anything. He looked so smug I could not bear to look at him.

"I found us an even better deal," he announced. "Unbeatable deal."

"Whatever," my sister said. "No comment."

"The girls are spoiled," Mother muttered. "More interested in their own friends than going home to see the family."

My sister underlined a passage in her vocabulary workbook. "I'm the one who cancelled my Mexico trip."

"Why do we have to go back to China now?" I asked. "Why not during the summer when we all have more time?"

"This is a good deal," Father repeated.

I can't leave. When I come back, it will all be over. But that was ridiculous. I was thirteen years old and completely under their control. I had no choice.

I did not look up. It frightened me that I was capable of hating my own father for even an instant. "I'll go," I said. "Seriously, I'll go. No more complaints."

At midnight on some evening in mid-December, out of the corner of my eye, I noticed a flickering from Josie's window across the street. A flashlight, turning on and off. Though it seemed arbitrary at first, there was something vaguely deliberate in the pattern. As I studied the pauses and the first dim speculations stirred in my gut, I forced my gaze back down at my textbook. No, I simply would not think such things. Nothing could possibly come out of it. I had a final exam the next day. For a few minutes, I could not lift my eyes off the page, for fear that the flickering had stopped, for fear that indeed, I had imagined it all. Or worse, or perhaps better, the light was indeed flickering for someone, but not me. Some lucky soul. Without looking, I reached up to turn the knob which shut the mini-blind slats, but as I did, a rumbling came from the street, and I jerked my head up instinctively: the lights again, and they *were* flickering at me.

I leapt up from my books and dashed down the stairs, out the door and through the wet grass, tripping across the garden hose. All these years, and neither of us had ever crossed the road into the property of the other.

She was sitting on her knees in the grass, motionless for a second, like a lawn statue.

"It's about time," she said. "I've only been sending you messages every night."

"What are we going to do?"

"What are we going to do? We're going for a bike ride, of course."

This was not exactly what I had wanted. I wanted her to say she had written a script for a new play, that we were going inside to rehearse it, that I would see her every night for the rest of the week and that she would speak to me in school, ask me to sit at her table during lunch and call me over to her locker in the hall. I wanted her to say that when the snow did come, it would not change anything and that even if I left for China and stayed there for three weeks, she would be waiting for me when I returned. I wanted to say . . . But I said nothing.

Emerging from the garage with her bike, Josie flung one leg over the seat and slid her foot into the pedal, then circled around me twice.

"Jump on back."

Then we were streaming through the neighborhood, and I made a quick prayer that the day and night would reverse themselves, or that night would consume the day, burn it away, so that nothing remained but one endless stretch of night. And so we rode in the night that was not night—past the MacKenzies and the Lowrys and the Robertsons and the Thompsons, Josie's ponytail scratching my neck, wisps of hair in my face, tassels fluttering on the handlebars, bicycle beneath us like a swift-flowing vessel down that black river of a road. All lit up, the neighborhood was like a giant felled traffic light, the driveways and mailboxes awash in the red-green-yellow glow. As we sped down, I smelled something burning faintly, heard a crackling noise that sounded like a fly being zapped. The streets flickered around me, and the bicycle spokes spun between my legs. I had the sensation that I was stuck in a film, reappearing and disappearing with every frame, everything made anew with every blink. When we reached the edge of the neighborhood, the large stone sign (Fo-wood Court) still missing its "x," we turned out into the main road, with its one-level houses, where it was empty, save for the distant rumble of a truck. Why was no one else out on a night like this? We rode out into the middle of the road, right over the yellow line. I looked up at the black sky overhead and thought of how much space there was, how much world to decorate. Then Josie pedaled backyards, spun around, and we were in the woods again, riding down a bike path I had never known existed. Though it was much darker here, I recognized the backyards of a few homes in which I had played as a child many years ago, in another life. We passed through a clearing into the Jordans' backyard, rolled up and over a hill and stopped beneath a badminton net. We climbed off and let the bicycle fall against a tree stump. The pool, sunken in from the deck, with its patio table and folded umbrella, was smaller than I expected.

Josie yawned. "I'm exhausted now, but some other night, you will have to come over for a swim."

"I'm going to China in a few days," I said. "I won't be back until mid-January."

I had not seen her stop and pick it up, but she was tossing a shuttlecock up and down now, her back facing me. She was quiet for a long time. Then she spoke in a small voice. "I'm moving away this spring. You know that, right? Man, I'm so excited. I love Florida."

I did not wait for her to turn around before I muttered that it was late and that I had to go.

❦

The next morning, an anonymous opinion article was placed in the town newsletter: "Do People Have Too Much Time On Their Hands?" The article argued for a town curfew and for a greater amount of homework to be issued in school. It urged for a return to calmer days of black nights and clear lawns and sunrises whose effects were not diminished by the remembered violence of the lights. By drawing attention to the epidemic of insomnia that had overtaken the town, the article suggested that the demonic lights were draining the energy of those who feasted their eyes on its brilliance and engaged in the activities it encouraged. If one was suffering from insomnia, listlessness, manic energy, consumptive pallor, decreased analytical skill, or increased sex drive (three symptoms were enough for a doctor to prescribe a weekend in the mountains), he was most likely a victim of light pollution and might recuperate in the nearby Candlelight Resort, where patients were treated to a week without electricity.

A few days later, a professor of sociology (Shelly Watson of the local technology institute) issued a study which analyzed the effect of peer pressure on the lighting craze and provided tips on how one might resist the costly, time-consuming, and potentially hazardous activity. Around this time, pairs of Dark Goggles became popular among conservatives and were worn even during the day to express adherence to the movement. Unfortunately for detractors of the lights, the articles merely romanticized the decadence of the families with the most brilliant displays and those teenagers who stayed awake all night, mingling in the streets, watching the performances, playing drinking games, and making love in the shadows. They were nicknamed Light Addicts and Children of the Flames. A local advertisement for Lite beer featured a man and woman floating and fornicating in a glass of beer whose bubbles were tiny lights. The caption below read "Be A Lite Addict" in flaming letters. A week later, when a heartbroken teenager committed suicide by hanging himself with a circuit of Christmas lights, the newspapers received hundreds of letters expressing concern over the dangerous trend. Though the public suicide caused a few light supporters to retreat from the streets, it also prompted the appearance of "Lucifer Lights," lights that burst into flames after a pre-programmed amount of time. Though they were illegal, they could be purchased on the black market and were an ever-popular decoration at the parties of rowdy teenagers and college students (at a fraternity party, it was said, a pledge was wrapped in Lucifer Lights and made to serve as a human torch). In our neighborhood, these articles had the paradoxical effect of producing the most outrageous lighting displays any of us had ever seen. As electricity bills skyrocketed, the displays grew so bright, they were brighter than the brightest summer day, brighter than the highest noon and the most radiant snow, and soon some of the most passionate defenders of the lights began to leave their own houses dark for a few hours every night. One by one, I knew, they would all dim.

"I told you," Mother said during dinner on the eve of our trip to China. "I told you it would come. You just can't hold it back."

"Perhaps it's a good thing we're going away for Christmas then." I didn't look up. "It's always nice to come back in mid-January after all the undecorating is done. You miss the bad part."

Mother blew lightly on a piece of meat she had pierced with a chopstick: "So much trouble. Those damn lights, they're all just going to take them down, just as I predicted."

The next morning, we left for Shanghai. In all the years that followed, I never spoke to Josie again.

Acknowledgments ❧

"Winter Memories of the Summer Bear" won the 2007 American Short Fiction short story contest and appeared in *American Short Fiction*, Summer 2007 (Vol. 10, Issue 38).

"Stricken" appeared in *Bellingham Review* as the first-place winner of the 2006 Tobias Wolff Award.

"Animal Control" appeared in *The Potomac Review*, Fall 2007 (Issue 42).

"The Chorus" appeared in *enRoute*, a Canadian in-flight magazine affiliated with Air Canada, in 2006.

"Joyless Men" appeared in *Water~Stone Review*, Fall 2007.

"The Report" appeared in *American Short Fiction*, Fall 2007.

"Carker" was originally published in *The Georgia Review*, Summer 2007 (Vol. LXI, Number 2).

Thanks to the editors of these journals.

Contributors' Biographies ❦

JACOB M. APPEL is a graduate of the MFA Creative Writing Program at New York University. His short fiction appears in *Alaska Quarterly Review*, *Missouri Review*, *Southwest Review*, *Threepenny Review*, and elsewhere. He can be found on the web at www.jacobmappel.com, and he answers email at jacobmappel@gmail.com.

MIRIAM GERSHOW is a writer and teacher living in Eugene, Oregon. Her stories appear in *Black Warrior Review*, *Quarterly West*, *Gulf Coast*, and elsewhere. Her first novel, *The Local News*, is forthcoming from Spiegel & Grau.

NICK HEALY is a writer and editor in Mankato, Minnesota. His stories appear in *Speakeasy*, *Water~Stone Review*, *Great River Review*, *Broken Bridge Review*, *The Blueroad Reader*, and elsewhere. He has an MFA in Creative Writing from Minnesota State University, Mankato, and he is a 2008 recipient of an Artist Initiative Grant from the Minnesota State Arts Board.

BRODIE SMITH received a B.A. in literature from the University of Texas at Austin and a B.S. in mathematics from the University of Texas at Dallas. "Watch Him Burn" is his first publication. He currently lives in Richardson, Texas, and is working on a novel.

Born in Vancouver, ERIN SOROS is the Charles Pick writer-in-residence at the University of East Anglia in England, where she is completing her first novel. She has published poetry, fiction and non-fiction, most recently in *The Indiana Review* and *The Iowa Review*. "The Chorus" was produced for the CBC as winner of the national CBC Literary Award for Short Fiction. In 2006, another story was produced for BBC Radio as winner of the Commonwealth Prize for the Short Story. In 2008, she was a finalist for the BBC National Short Story Award.

"Winter Memories of the Summer Bear" is the title story of KIMBERLY WILLARDSON's collection, each story of which features bears. Kimberly served as editor for *The Vincent Brothers Review* from 1988 until 2004, when she moved from Ohio to North Carolina. She is at work on her first novel.

NAOMI WILLIAMS has an MA in Creative Writing from UC Davis. A recent Pushcart Prize winner, her short fiction appears in *The Southern Review*, *American Short Fiction*, *The Gettysburg Review*, *ZYZZYVA*, and *Colorado Review*. She lives with her family in Davis, California.

MARK WISNIEWSKI has won a Pushcart Prize, the 2006 Cattarulla Award, the 2006 Tobias Wolff Award, a 2006 Isherwood Foundation Fellowship in Fiction, and the 2007 Gival Press Short Story Award. He is the author of the novel *Confessions of a Polish Used Car Salesman*, the short-story collection *All Weekend With the Lights On*, and the book of narrative poems *One of Us One Night*. His stories appear in *The Southern Review*, *Virginia Quarterly Review*, *Triquarterly*, *Antioch Review*, *Glimmer Train*, *The Missouri Review*, *The Gettysburg Review*, *Boulevard*, *Mississippi Review*, *The Sun*, *New England Review*, and elsewhere.

CHRISTINA YU recently received an MFA in Creative Writing from the University of Notre Dame where she was the Diversity Fellow, the Sparks Summer Fellow at Hachette Book Group, and captain of the water polo team. In 2005, she received an A.B in English from Dartmouth College where she won the Perkins Prize for excellence in English and was named a finalist for the Rhodes Scholarship. Her fiction appears in *Gargoyle* and *Indiana Review*.

DEL SOL PRESS, based out of Washington, D.C., publishes exemplary and edgy fiction, poetry, and nonfiction (mostly contemporary, with the occasional reprint). Founded in 2002, the press sponsors two annual competitions:

THE DEL SOL PRESS POETRY PRIZE is a yearly book-length competition with a January deadline for an unpublished book of poems.

THE ROBERT OLEN BUTLER FICTION PRIZE is awarded for the best short story, published or unpublished. The deadline is in November of each year.

http://www.delsolpress.org